Helen O Donnell

Sacristan's Guide

A handbook for altar societies and others having charge of the altar and sanctuary

Helen O Donnell

Sacristan's Guide
A handbook for altar societies and others having charge of the altar and sanctuary

ISBN/EAN: 9783741192210

Manufactured in Europe, USA, Canada, Australia, Japa

Cover: Foto ©Andreas Hilbeck / pixelio.de

Manufactured and distributed by brebook publishing software
(www.brebook.com)

Helen O Donnell

Sacristan's Guide

SACRISTAN'S GUIDE.

A HANDBOOK FOR ALTAR SOCIETIES AND
OTHERS HAVING CHARGE OF THE
ALTAR AND SANCTUARY.

BY

A MEMBER OF AN ALTAR SOCIETY

New York, Cincinnati, Chicago:

BENZIGER BROTHERS,

PRINTERS TO THE
HOLY APOSTOLIC SEE

PUBLISHERS OF
BENZIGER'S MAGAZINE

JULY 22, 1884.

Miss Helen O'Donnell:

I very willingly give the Imprimatur which you ask. The examination of the MS. and its approval by the Reverend gentlemen named in your note are guarantee that it may safely, and with profit, be placed in the hands of the public.

I remain,

Very respectfully,

Your obedient servant,

✠ Francis,

Bishop of Albany.

CONTENTS.

6 *Contents.*

CHAPTER I.

General Remarks.

HE custom of adorning the altar is one of great antiquity, as is proved by the frequent reference made to it by early ecclesiastical writers; and their commendation of those engaged in the pious work is sufficient evidence that they regarded it as a practice worthy of emulation.

St. Jerome furnishes a good example of this in speaking of the zealous Nepotian, " whose pious care," he says, " was such that he made flowers of many kinds, and the leaves of trees, and the branches of the vine contribute to the beauty and ornament of the Church." " These things," continues the Saint, " were indeed but trifling in themselves, but a pious mind devoted to Christ is intent upon small things as well as great, and neglects nothing that pertains even to the meanest office of the Church."

St. Augustine also relates in his touching account of the conversion of Martialis to Christianity, shortly before death, "that his son-in-law, after praying with much fervor at the foot of the altar, carried off from it some of the flowers placed there to convey them to the bedside of his dying relative."

The custom of decoration in the days of primitive Christianity was, however, but a continuation of that practised by the Jews in the ornamentation of their tabernacle and altar, which, in obedience to the command given to Moses by God Himself, they beautified not only with cherubim and candlesticks and lamps of pure gold, rich cloths of service and embroidered hangings, but they brought also "the fir-tree, and the pine-tree, and the box together to adorn My sanctuary."

The adornment of the altar, however, is only *one* branch of the high and holy work devolving on those having the altar and sanctuary in charge. Many and varied are the duties appertaining thereto, some of which are of a very practical nature, but, if discharged in the proper spirit, represent a sentiment as beautiful as that expressed in the weaving of garlands or the decking of shrines.

In Catholic countries ladies of the highest rank * deem it an honor to be *allowed* to perform even the most menial service (if such it can be called) around the altar. In this country, on the contrary, there are some who seem to consider it degrading to do anything within the sanctuary save the ornamental work, leaving the really important part to be done by persons hired for the purpose.

Now this is an idea entirely at variance with the spirit of Catholicity. The work of the altar should be a labor of love, "without money and without price," and no true lady need be ashamed to do the necessary sweeping, cleaning, or dusting within the sanctuary.

Another erroneous idea, and one which deters many persons from assisting in the work of the altar, is that it is a difficult undertaking, requiring much taste and skill on the part of those engaged in it. Let no one hold back on this account, as there is scarcely any one who has not sufficient taste, if properly cultivated, and nothing better tends to develop it than a careful study of the rubrics relating to the care of the altar and surroundings. In fact,

---

* Princess Isabella, the daughter of the Emperor of Brazil, is said to spend much time each week in sweeping and cleaning the church, considering it a privilege to thus employ herself.

they leave very little scope for the exercising of *individual taste*, providing as they do for the smallest detail connected with Divine worship, investing it with a beautiful symbolism which is often utterly lost, however, through the neglect or indifference of those having the altar in charge.

To illustrate the truth of this the following incident of recent occurrence is given.

In a church where there is a large and flourishing society of the Perpetual Lamp, the object of which is to keep a taper continually burning before the altar of the Sacred Heart, the pastor was one Sunday expatiating on the beauties and benefits of this devotion, and urging such of the congregation as did not already belong to the society to be enrolled without delay. The attention of his hearers was naturally attracted to the altar in question, when, behold ! the lamp was indeed there, but the " perpetual light" had gone out, owing to the "foolish virgins" having forgotten to trim it ; and not only that, but the sanctuary lamp was likewise in eclipse.

Too much importance cannot be attached to the strict observance of the rubric which enjoins that "everything be done decently and in order." Therefore care should be taken that all preparations are made in due season and according to the prescribed law, employing no substitutes in the sanctuary for specified furniture, and allowing nothing unsightly (however convenient) a place therein.

The care of the altar is a religious duty necessarily tending to excite devotion and reverence in the heart of the worker, whose natural impulse it should be to perform her labors in a quiet, recollected manner befitting the sacred character of the offices she is privileged to discharge. In fact, it is the *silent worker* who accomplishes the most, providing all things needful beforehand, so that there may be no lack of requisite articles, or confusion occasioned by tardy preparations, to mar the solemnity of any service or function.

"Cleanliness is the handmaid of beauty"—a maxim that members of altar societies should put into daily practice by seeing that the sanctuary is at all times exquisitely neat and clean.

WHERE AND HOW TO BUY CHURCH GOODS.

Have a catalogue of church goods always at hand, and look it carefully over before ordering anything in that line, and in doing so bear in mind that the *best is always the cheapest* in goods of this kind, as in dry-goods. Cheap goods are often a necessity, but they are unprofitable, serving only in emergencies, and having to be replaced in a short time. Therefore, where it is possible, only the *very best* should be purchased ; and if that is out of the question, at least a medium quality should be selected, but never the *poorest*, except in extreme cases, and then with the expectation of getting something better at the earliest opportunity.

Where a society intends buying a large bill of goods, it is an excellent idea to send one or more members of good judgment direct to the manufactory or place where such goods are sold. Very often a personal inspection will result in getting some articles, if not all, of a better quality than had been intended.

If this is not practicable, however, it is perfectly safe to send an order to some reliable firm, resting assured that it will be filled in a satisfactory manner.

Dealers will also, if desired, send photographs of complete sets of vestments of which only parts are shown in the catalogue, so there will be no difficulty in making a selection, and no chance for disappointment afterwards.

But whether a purchase be large or small, consisting of an entire outfit of vestments and altar furniture, or of *only a few yards of silk, lace, gold fringe, braid, emblems, or other trim-*

mings, it is recommended that societies procure them at a house dealing *only in church goods*, as it is almost impossible to get them of suitable quality and design elsewhere.

Parties make a great mistake in supposing— as they sometimes do—that they can have many of these articles made cheaper at home. This is proved by the experience of a clergyman who, from motives of economy, employed a man skilled in ornamental wood-work to make him a baptismal-font of black walnut, he (the clergyman) drawing the design for it. When finished it was a very handsome piece of workmanship; but what was his chagrin to discover that the font had cost fifteen dollars more than he would have paid for a much finer one at a place where such goods are manufactured expressly for the use of the Church!

Many similar examples might be cited showing the advantage of ascertaining the cost of the various articles used in the church service from a dealer therein, before purchasing elsewhere, or, like the good Father referred to above, having them made at additional expense and trouble.

CHAPTER II.

𝔉urniture and 𝔒rnaments 𝔑ecessary for the 𝔄ltar and 𝔖anctuary.

𝔗he 𝔄ltar.

LINING OF THE TABERNACLE.

THE rubric requires that the tabernacle be lined with white silk or satin.

This lining may be smoothly put on, and fastened at the top and bottom with small silver-headed tacks; the whole interior, roof, sides, and floor, being entirely covered.

If the tabernacle is of marble or stone, it should have an inner tabernacle * of wood, to avoid dampness and mould, and this, too, should be silk-lined.

INNER VEIL OF THE TABERNACLE.

A veil is likewise required to hang just inside the tabernacle door. This veil should be

---

* It might, perhaps, be more properly termed a lining of wood.

also of silk or satin, and *invariably white, no other color being allowed* at any time.

It is generally open in the middle (although, it may be in one piece, if desired), and accord-ing to the taste and ingenuity of the maker can be more or less elaborate, having a border of gold embroidery on both edges, or simply dotted over with spangles or spears of gold wheat. The materials of which it is made, however, should be of the very best quality, and the embroidery on it exquisitely done, as nothing cheap or commonplace should be allowed in or around the tabernacle.

A rich thread or blond lace might be put on the edge for a finish, though gold fringe is often used.

The best method of putting the veil in place * is to attach it to a slender silver rod of the proper length, by means of silver rings or loops of silk cord, and fasten it firmly with small sil-ver staples over the tabernacle door (on the inside). Little knobs or screws on each end of the rod will prevent it slipping from side to side.

---

* In the same manner that curtains are hung—the inner veil of the tabernacle being in fact a curtain.

2

THE DOOR OF THE TABERNACLE.

The door of the tabernacle—if of wood— must also be lined with white silk or satin, which may be neatly pasted on around the edges or fastened on with silver-headed tacks, though the former is the better way. An appropriate emblem, or the letters I. H. S., can be embroidered in the centre of the lining.

CANDLESTICKS.

Although the rubric requires a different number of candlesticks (as also of candles) for different occasions, there is still a certain number seen on every altar—whatever the service— that may be properly regarded as stationary furniture.

These are the *six large candlesticks* (usually of varnished brass) which are placed on the top step of the altar, three on each side of the tabernacle, and which are from fifteen to fifty inches high, in proportion to the size of the altar.*

---

* In ordering candlesticks (or in fact any ornaments or furniture for the altar or sanctuary, unless one is quite certain of what is wanted), it is a good idea to state the dimensions and style of architecture of the altar for which they are intended, and the dealer will probably know just what is

While six candlesticks will answer require-
ments as far as this particular kind is concerned,
yet very few altars are considered properly furnished without twelve, and in many cases
eighteen, in three different sizes.

Of course everything like overcrowding
should be avoided, but at least two rows of
these tall candlesticks are necessary on the
majority of altars to preserve a symmetrical
effect—one row being apt to give a top-heavy
appearance, especially when set in a straight
line. *

As the candles in these candlesticks are only
lighted at High Mass and Vespers (generally
speaking), it is customary to have two or four
—as the case may require—smaller candlesticks
on the bottom step for Low Masses and other
functions.

Besides these, from two to five pairs of candelabra will be necessary for the adornment of
the altar on Sundays and festivals, and they
also should be of various sizes and styles, yet
in harmony with the other ornaments thereon.

---

suitable. Mention particularly the width of the steps on
which the candlesticks are to be placed, as it is important to
have them the right size in that respect, for if too large they
are always in danger of slipping off.

* To be strictly rubrical they should graduate upward to
the cross.

Quite a number of smaller candle-holders, either metal or china, will be wanted for special occasions when the altar is to be illuminated.

Several pairs of silver candlesticks (plain or branched) will be required to complete the assortment, together with six or eight large *requiem candlesticks* for placing around the catafalque at funerals and requiem Masses, and six of a smaller size for the altar on like occasions.

ACOLYTE CANDLESTICKS, TORCHES, AND LANTERNS.

A pair of large candlesticks and six torches must be provided for the acolytes; and in churches where processions on Corpus Christi and such festivals take place in the open air, six processional lanterns are almost indispensable, as the least breath of wind extinguishes the ordinary torch, thereby rendering it unfit for carrying out of doors.

PASCHAL CANDLESTICK.

The Paschal candlestick, as its name indicates, is used for the purpose of holding the Paschal or Easter candle. As only one such candlestick is required, it should be as handsome as possible, and in keeping with the other ornaments used during this solemn festival-time.

There are several styles of this candlestick to be found, the most appropriate being white, ornamented with gold. Something quite new in this line is a candlestick of zinc, painted and beautifully decorated to correspond with the Paschal candle, which is now generally decorated. A richly-gilded candlestick, however, will answer very well for the purpose.

TENEBRÆ CANDLESTICK.

One tenebræ or triangular candlestick for Holy Week, as also a reed for the triple candle carried on Holy Saturday.

THE SANCTUARY LAMP.

In former times it was customary to have three or five lamps burning before the altar of the Blessed Sacrament, but at the present day one suffices.

It is suspended from the ceiling at such an elevation as to shed its rays directly on the tabernacle.

BRACKET-LAMPS.

These lamps are much used in the sanctuary nowadays, affording the light so much needed during evening service, when the altar is only partially illuminated. Four or six of them would answer for an ordinary-sized sanctuary.

CRUCIFIX AND PROCESSIONAL CROSS. -

According to the ceremonial of bishops, the crucifix in the middle of the altar (on the tabernacle) should be similar in material and design to the candlesticks between which it is placed. In compliance with this law it is usually made to correspond with them in all their various styles, and should be selected with due regard to this important fact.

The processional cross can likewise be had to match the crucifix.

MISSAL-STANDS.

Rubricians designate a cushion as the proper resting-place for the missal when on the altar, but custom and convenience sanction the use of a book-stand instead.

Several new and elegant styles of missalstands have been lately introduced, which like many church ornaments of the present day surpass in beauty and workmanship anything in that line heretofore seen. Among those especially worthy of mention are revolving stands, stands on wheels, brass and gilt stands

richly set with stones, and black-walnut stands
of Gothic form, either plain or handsomely
carved.

For every-day use, however, the ordinary
black-walnut stand retains favor as being the
most serviceable.

In churches where there are side-altars several smaller missal-stands must be provided, as
also missals of a corresponding size.

ABLUTION-CUP.

An *ablution-cup* of metal or glass in which
the priest may purify his fingers must be always
on the altar.   It should be kept about half full
of water.

ALTAR-CARDS.

One set of handsome altar-cards, nicely
framed, will answer for Sundays, together with
a set of plainer ones for week-day services.

If there be side-altars, one or two additional
sets of smaller-sized cards must be furnished
for them, and another set mounted on paste-
board will be found useful in churches where
the clergymen attend stations or missions in
outlying districts.

CRUETS.

It will be necessary to have several sets of
cruets suitable for different occasions.   The

great convenience resulting from the use of glass ones, the transparency of which enables the celebrant to readily distinguish the water from the wine, has caused them to receive the preference over all others.

Silver cruets, however, or those of cut glass with silver or gold plate and mountings, are rather more appropriate on handsomely-furnished altars.

RELIQUARIES.

Churches fortunate in the possession of sacred relics should have them properly encased in reliquaries, of which very handsome designs are now seen. In Rome there are usually four on the altar, two on each side, placed between the candlesticks.

STATUARY.

No altar is really complete in its appointments without a statue of an adoring angel on the pedestal at each side of the tabernacle. These angels, however, need not be stationary, but can be removed on occasions when other statuary might be more appropriate.

THABOR, OR EXPOSITION.

Altars that have not an upper tabernacle, or throne of exposition, should have a *Thabor* on

which the Blessed Sacrament can be elevated
at Benediction or during the Forty Hours'
Adoration.

The Thabor is something quite new and very
ornamental, supplying a long-felt want for something of the kind on which the monstrance can
be raised to a proper height.

ARTIFICIAL FLOWERS AND PLANTS.

Flowers and plants are an important feature
in the decoration of the altar, and as far as
possible only natural ones should be used, as
it is not for their beauty alone that they are
thus employed, but because their fragrance is
deemed a fitting incense breathed out before
the tabernacle of the Holy of Holies.

As it is difficult to obtain them at certain
seasons (that is, in some localities), it is well to
be provided with a supply of artificial flowers,
plants, and vines, which, as far as appearances
are concerned, will serve very acceptably in
their stead. In fact, they have now attained
such a state of perfection that it is hard to distinguish between them and natural ones.

Some of these artificial flowers are tastefully
arranged in bouquets, set in handsome vases;
while others are in the form of plants, having
the appearance of actually growing in the orna-

mental pots in which they are placed. A striking contrast to the stiff and ungainly imitations
of nature that adorned (?) our altars in the
past.

An altar should have from three to six pairs
of bouquets, and the same number of plants (of
various kinds). These, if necessary, may be
mixed or interspersed with natural flowers and
used to good advantage in decorations on fes-
tival-days.

VASES AND FLOWER-POTS

Of gold, silver, brass, china, and porcelain—
both plain and ornamental—are used on altars,
though taste would suggest that nothing in-
congruous or out of harmony with the prescribed altar ornaments be placed thereon.

It is preferable to have a smaller number of
vases that are at once beautiful and appropriate
to the place, than to have a great many of a
cheap and tawdry kind. Besides, tall, slender
glasses are in much favor for holding cluster-
bouquets, which, together with the baskets so
generally used for flowers nowadays, render an
array of vases unnecessary.

EWER AND BASIN.

It is necessary to have a small ewer and basin
of silver, britannia, or glass, though they are

rarely used, save when the bishop or some such dignitary officiates, the cruet-stand ordinarily answering the purpose of the washing of hands at the lavabo.

CHIMES AND GONGS.

Brass, silver, and nickel-plated chimes and gongs are now manufactured expressly for the use of the Church. A set of chimes produce a very sweet harmony, but gongs are better adapted for a large edifice, being more distinctly heard at a distance from the altar. A small hand-bell will also be wanted, together with several clappers for Holy Week services.

The Sanctuary.

CARPETING.

In selecting a carpet for the sanctuary two things are to be considered, durability and color, as it is important it should be of a quality that will stand the constant wear to which it will be subjected, and of colors that will not fade.

A cheney pattern with a rich border is recommended as being both handsome and economical. It can be cut to fit around the altar-steps more easily and with better effect than a larger-figured carpet could be, and has, moreover, the advantage of harmonizing with the many-hued vestments worn in the sanctuary, which is a great point in its favor. Another style of carpet that looks very well is one having a fine running vine in bright colors on a ground of neutral tint.

English body Brussels or Axminster is generally used, and should always be double-lined, but three-ply ingrain * will be found very serviceable, especially in small sanctuaries.

Where the flooring and steps in the sanctuary are of inlaid wood—as is sometimes the case—a rich rug for the platform (predella) of the altar will be required, together with strips of stair-carpeting, corresponding with it in color and design, for the steps in front of the altar and at each side. These strips should be *securely* fastened down to avoid accidents.

SANCTUARY SEATS.

Regarding seats in the sanctuary, the rubric says:

" There should be no chairs in the sanctuary except that of the bishop or some very distin-

---

* Many clergymen of acknowledged taste in such matters declare three-ply ingrain preferable to any other kind of carpeting for the sanctuary.

guished personage. Priests, even canons, and others belonging to the clergy should sit on benches. These should be neatly made with high backs, especially when attached to the walls. The bench for the celebrant should be near the Epistle side, and should be sufficiently large to accommodate the celebrant, deacon, and subdeacon.

"It may be richly ornamented with carved work, but should never look like a throne. . . .

"This bench should be about seven feet long and covered with baize—green for ordinary occasions, and purple when the vestments are purple. When they are black, however, it should be *uncovered*."

In many churches in this country, the celebrant's seat (or as it is called in the rubric, the bench of the sacred ministers) is in accordance with the above rule regarding form, but is seldom seen with the covering prescribed, being generally upholstered in leather, cloth, or plush, sometimes brown and oftentimes red—a striking disregard of a rule which is more easily observed than violated, since the baize covering referred to is certainly much less expensive than the rich upholstery displayed in many sanctuaries.

An ordinary high-backed chair will answer for the celebrant's seat, and two smaller ones of a similar style for that of the deacon and subdeacon, where it is *impossible* to get a suit-able " bench" made.

These chairs, however, should have coverings of the required colors and material.

Benches or stalls are also to be provided for other clergy, and for the acolytes.

In our churches it is customary to have, in-stead of benches, a few reserved chairs for visit-ing clergymen, and small camp-chairs for the acolytes and sanctuary-boys, the preference being given to chairs of the latter kind, on ac-count of the great convenience of folding them up and putting them aside on occasions when more space is wanted in the sanctuary.

Altar Societies are not expected to provide the chairs (nor many other articles used in the sanctuary), but they are here enumerated, as it may sometimes be necessary to see that they are procured and put into place.

THE CREDENCE.

The credence is the table on which the nec-essary articles for the sacred functions are placed.   It should be four and a half feet long, three feet wide (if the size of the sanctuary will admit), and three feet high.   If stationary, it should correspond in general style with the rest of the sanctuary furniture; but if not, it can be made of any light wood and painted white.

The appropriate place for the credence is on the Epistle side of the sanctuary, and—if there be sufficient room—against the side-wall, as the rubric positively forbids its *resting against the altar*.

For any of the services at which the credence is used it is required to be covered with white linen, which must hang to the floor on every side. It is not allowable to decorate it in any manner with flowers, vines, crosses, or other emblems.

It should be covered only when in use.

Small stands are frequently substituted for the credence in sanctuaries where economy of space is a necessity, and they also should have a covering of white linen.

THE AMBRY.

The ambry, or tabernacle for holding the holy oils, is generally fastened to the wall of the sanctuary on the Gospel side, although it is sometimes hung in the sacristy.

Ambries can be found to correspond with the architecture of different altars, Roman, Gothic, etc.—a fact which in purchasing should not be forgotten.

PRIE-DIEU.

Two or more kneeling-desks will be required in proportion to the number of clergymen connected with the church. Those of black walnut upholstered with green silk plush are appropriate for the sanctuary;* while for common use in the sacristy those of oak or some such wood are more suitable. A prie-dieu and confessional combined is still better for the latter place.

LECTERNS.

At least three lecterns will be necessary in a church where Holy Week ceremonies are celebrated, and it will not be amiss to have a few additional ones in case they are wanted.

All articles or furniture of wood used in the sanctuary should be uniform in color.

BALDACHIN.

Among the many new and beautiful articles intended for use and ornament in and around the sanctuary is the baldachin—a portable shrine or niche for statuary.

It is made of various kinds of wood, hand-

---

* The prie-dieu properly belongs in the sacristy, though there are occasions when it is used in the sanctuary.

somely carved, and can be had either white, colored, or richly gilded, and of a design to accord with other sanctuary furniture.

When stationary it is fastened to the wall, but can be carried in procession if desired.

PISCINA.

This is a receptacle on the Epistle side of the sanctuary, with a pipe attached for carrying off the water in which the priest washes the chalice linens, the remains of the baptismal water, etc It generally has a shelf in the top for holding the cruets of water and wine.

The piscina should *never be used except for the purpose intended*, nor should other kinds of water be poured into it.

3

CHAPTER III.

𝕷𝖎𝖓𝖊𝖓𝖘 𝖀𝖘𝖊𝖉 𝕺𝖓 𝖆𝖓𝖉 𝕬𝖗𝖔𝖚𝖓𝖉 𝖙𝖍𝖊 𝕬𝖑𝖙𝖆𝖗.

𝕬𝖑𝖙𝖆𝖗=𝕮𝖑𝖔𝖙𝖍𝖘.

ACCORDING to the rubric, every altar on which the Holy Sacrifice is of-fered up must have *three* linen cov-erings besides the crismale * or wax-cloth that is fastened over the altar-stone.

The first *two* cloths entirely cover the table of the altar, while the *third* and upper one must be large enough to cover *them*, and hang down on both sides so as to nearly touch the floor, unless the altar is in the form of a sarcophagus, in which case it is sufficient if it covers the altar surface all around.

These three coverings are symbolical of the Blessed Trinity, and are also used in commem-oration of the linen cloths in which the body of our Divine Saviour was wrapped when He was laid in the sepulchre, while the wax-cloth typifies the seal that was set on the stone placed

---

* This cloth should never be disturbed, as its purpose is to secure or preserve the consecrated oils that have been solemnly placed in the altar by the bishop.

at the door. The *altar-stone* itself represents Calvary.

The altar-cloths should be of fine but heavy linen, cut so as to fit around the tabernacle, and neatly hemmed. The front edge and ends, being straight, can have a hem an inch and a half wide, but the back, which is uneven, will admit of a very narrow one only.

As a general thing they are perfectly plain, but there is no objection to the upper one being embroidered or trimmed with lace. On the contrary, it is often seen in religious houses, as well as in some churches, ornamented with exquisite needlework.

It can also have five crosses, worked with white, one in the centre and one in each corner.

Buttonholes may be made, crosswise, in the hem on the front edge of the second cloth, to which the lace ruffle can be attached by means of buttons about eight or ten inches apart.

After the altar-cloths are thus prepared they must be blessed by a bishop or some one authorized by him.

Chalice Linens.

CORPORAL.

The corporal should be made of fine linen, about twenty inches square, with a hem half an inch wide around it, and edged with thread lace an inch and a half wide, or thereabouts.

It is folded four times, thus dividing it into nine squares, and in the centre of the middle square, on the fore part, a small red cross must be worked.

The corporal is spread on the altar under the chalice at Mass, and is also placed under the monstrance at Benediction, besides serving to hold the consecrated particles ; it derives its name from the body of our Lord thus resting on it.

The rules regarding this sacred cloth are so strict that *no laic is allowed to handle it after use*, and it must therefore be washed when necessary, by a priest or clerk in Holy Orders. After it has been carefully washed by him in *three waters* the society can have it done up with the other linens.

Once having been used at Mass, the corporal is kept in the burse. A special one should be kept with the bread for the Blessed Sacrament whereon to set the monstrance.

PURIFICATOR.

The purificator is also of linen, and is eighteen inches long and twelve wide, having a hem half an inch wide all around, and a cross in the middle.

It need *not* be blessed, although it *may;* but after use it cannot be handled by lay persons until it has been first washed by a cleric.

It is seldom trimmed with lace, for the reason that the lace is liable to catch on the ornaments of the chalice when the celebrant. is wiping it, for which purpose the purificator is used.

PALL.

The pall is five inches square, and is usually made of two pieces of linen sewed together on three sides (like a burse), the fourth or opening one being hemmed. Into this a piece of card-board is slipped to hold it stiff and firm. Sometimes, however, it is made of four thicknesses of linen starched very stiff, so as to dispense with the card-board; but the former is the better way of making it.

The pall should likewise have a small cross in the centre, and may be edged with narrow lace. In many convents and religious houses the chalice linens are made of linen cambric ornamented with costly lace, and in some cases have a border of hemstitching; but such are rather suitable for private chapels than for churches, where something more serviceable is needed.

It is well to have one or two handsomely-trimmed sets of these linens for extra occasions,

such as the visits of the bishop or other dis
tinguished prelates, and for great feasts.

COMMUNION-CLOTH.

Two feet is sufficiently wide for the com
munion-cloth, which must be of heavy linen.

The length of course depends on the size of
the altar-railing for which it is intended, and
to which it can be attached by means of hooks
fastened on the railing, a foot or so apart, with
loops of linen tape to correspond on the cloth ;
or buttonholes, if preferred, will do instead.

In some churches there is a wire running
round the railing to which the cloth is looped,
and when not in use it is drawn aside in folds.
This saves the trouble of putting it off and on,
but must necessarily expose it to greater wear.

Still another and very good way is to have
small brass or ivory knobs (such as are used in
hanging pictures) screwed on the rails, and the
cloth caught on them with loops of narrow
tape.

The communion-cloth can be made in two
or four sections, according to the size of the
railing, and have a hem two inches wide on the
lower edge, with one somewhat narrower on
the upper edge, and a still narrower one on the
sides.

LAVABO TOWEL.

The towel on which the priest wipes his fingers during Mass should be of linen, about thirty-six inches long and twenty-seven wide. It can be plain with the ends fringed, or be trimmed with lace.

CREDENCE-COVERING.

A very good arrangement in regard to covering the credence is to have a piece of white linen fitted to the top of the table, and a hem around it sufficiently wide to make a firm edge, on which buttons may be sewed about five inches apart. Then take a strip of linen wide enough to hang from the top of the table to the floor, and long enough to reach all around the table and lap over a little. On the lower edge (or bottom) of this strip put a hem an inch and a half wide, and a very narrow one on the upper edge, in which should be buttonholes to match the buttons on the top piece, to which it can be fastened. This will cover the table nicely, and can be quickly put on. An additional piece of linen will be required to complete it. This must be just the size of the table-top, and have a ruffle of lace around it which will hang over the edge. A few pins will hold it in place.

Two or three of these covers will be necessary, together with one or two smaller and plainer ones (i.e., without lace) to be used on Good Friday and Holy Saturday, when, according to the rubric, the cover must hang only a little over the edge of the table.

It is also well to have several covers of a suitable size for smaller tables or stands for week-day services. These may be edged with lace.

ALTAR-RUFFLES.

Altar-ruffles are not specified in the rubrics, but custom has rendered them almost indispensable, Good Friday being the only day on which they are excluded.

There are a great many kinds of ruffles appropriate for different occasions, varying in size from six to twenty-six inches in depth.

Every altar should be provided with at least two ruffles of thread lace for festivals. These should be of equal beauty, but quite different in style, as too much sameness in such things takes from the effect of altar-decorations, a diversity at times being pleasing to the eye.

Something comparatively new in ruffles is one of tulle embroidered with gold. In churches and convents in Europe it is no uncommon thing to see rare old laces glistening with gold, but until recently we have contented ourselves with imitations ingeniously devised by sticking on lace a design cut from gilt paper. Now, however, we have the real gold-lace ruffles, which impart a richness to the altar and are in keeping with the ornaments thereon.

For ordinary Sundays and holydays several ruffles of a plainer sort will be needed ; but they should not be of a *poor quality*, as cheap, coarse lace ought *never* to be put on the altar. Something quite simple will do for every-day use. In fact, the ladies of a society, if so disposed, could easily make a ruffle that would answer the purpose very well, by getting a plain Brussels lace, cutting it in strips of the required length, which could be neatly joined by overcasting the selvage edges together, and then darning a pretty design in it with linen floss, finishing it with a scallop on the edge. This will make a very nice ruffle at a trifling cost.

The ruffles on the side altars generally correspond with those on the high altar, though it is not important that they should.

Altar-ruffles are gathered, with a slight fulness, on a band of linen tape, on which buttons are sewed to match the buttonholes on the altar-cloths, to which they must be fastened.

Suitable lace for ruffles may be obtained where vestments are sold. Much of it is manufactured expressly for church purposes, having religious subjects and designs interwoven through it. ,

CHAPTER IV.

𝔙𝔢𝔰𝔱𝔪𝔢𝔫𝔱𝔰.

 " SET of vestments" consists of five pieces—the chasuble, stole, maniple, burse, and veil of the chalice; while a *complete set* for High Mass includes a dalmatic, stole, and maniple for the deacon, and a dalmatic * and maniple for the subdeacon.

A *complete High Mass set of purple* vestments has, besides the dalmatics, two additional chasubles and a large stole.

These extra chasubles are worn in Advent and Lent, and are termed *folded chasubles.*

The chasuble belonging to a *complete set* should not be worn at Low Masses, as it will soon grow shabby and look badly beside the dalmatics when worn at High Masses.

The vestments should be of rich materials:

---

* Formerly the dalmatic worn by the subdeacon was somewhat shorter than that of the deacon, and was called a tunic; but it is now the same length as the dalmatic, and is better known by that name.

silk, satin, velvet, and cloth of gold, handsomely or magnificently embroidered as occasion requires, with suitable trimmings and lined with silk, though muslin or cashmere can be used.

The vestments are in the five ecclesiastical colors, red, white, green, purple, and black, each color to be worn according to the sacred service or function.

Intermixing colors for the purpose of using one set of vestments for red, white, or green, instead of having a set of each color, *is forbidden. Cloth of gold*, however, can be used instead of *white.**

Although not included in a set of vestments, the alb, amice, and cincture properly belong to it, being equally important pieces in the vesture worn in the celebration of Mass.

The other vestments—cope, humeral veil, surplice (and stole for Benediction) are each separate and distinct pieces.

* In connection with these are the ornaments so-called, viz., veil of the tabernacle (also known as the canopy), antipendium, burse, and chalice veil or cover ; the two last named being included in a set of vestments.

They also are in the colors above mentioned, and should accord with the vestments in material and trimmings.

* Canons are privileged to wear cloth of gold for white red, or green

Description of Various Vestments—How they are to be Made, etc.

VESTMENTS WORN AT MASS.

The rubric requires that the alb be wholly of linen, the lace with which it is now ornamented being introduced at a later period, and, though authorized by custom, is still a mere accessory, and should never be used as a substitute for the linen, nor allowed to reach above the knees.

Except for ordinary wear, this lace should be of a rich quality, as common cotton lace is *unfit* for the sanctuary. This is demonstrated by the fact that lace-making * owes in a great

---

* All writers on the subject are unanimous in declaring this fact, one of them asserting that the "fine church lace of Spain was but little known to the commercial world of Europe until the dissolution of the Spanish monasteries (of which there were 8932) in 1830, when the most splendid specimens of nuns' work came suddenly into the market; not only the heavy lace designated *Spanish point*, but pieces of the finest description, so exquisite as to have been the work only of those whose 'time was not money,' and whose devotion to the Church rendered this work a labor of love."

Indeed, so closely connected with religion is lace making, that in a side-chapel in St. Peter's, Louvain, there is an altarpiece by Quentin Matsys, bearing the date 1495, which represents a girl engaged in making lace, presumably for the altar.

measure the perfection it attained centuries ago to the Church, which was at once its inspiration and munificent patron, the most exquisite specimens ever executed being made expressly for the service of the altar, and often from designs drawn by monks skilled with the pencil.

Where ladies have the time to do so, they can make the linen bodies of albs, buying for the bottoms laces which come in patterns expressly for the purpose. Where something handsome is desired Brussels lace is recommended (either for albs or surplices), though there are other kinds that are equally suitable.

Linen albs (without lace) are used in many churches in week-day services and for requiem Masses. They should be made of heavy linen, and according to the following dimensions, varying in size to suit the wearer: Six feet long and about twelve feet in circumference (at the bottom); the sleeves twenty-seven inches in length and seventeen in width at the top, narrowing towards the wrist like any other sleeve. The back, from shoulder to shoulder. should measure nearly one yard, across the chest the same, while the skirt must be gored to give sufficient fulness, and have a hem on the bottom four inches in width. The neck should be gathered a little in the back, and finished with a narrow band tied with linen tape. A hem an inch wide will answer down the front. It is important that albs or vestments of any kind should be well sewed and properly stayed.

Some rubricians are greatly in favor of albs having a border of embroidery around the bottom and on the sleeves, claiming that it is "far more in keeping with tradition and liturgy, besides being more artistic than any laces."

It would be a very easy matter to thus ornament them, as the market is full of embroidered edgings suitable for the purpose, although a better way would be for ladies skilled in needlework to embroider the edge of the alb itself.

The amice and cincture, like the alb, are of linen, the latter woven into a cord, while the former is a piece of fine cloth about thirty inches long and twenty wide. It is worn lengthwise on the shoulders, having strings of tape on the front corners with which to fasten it together.

It should have a hem nearly an inch wide all around, with a small red cross worked in the middle, about six inches from the upper edge.

THE CHASUBLE.

The chasuble is the outside vestment (having a cross on the back and a pillar in front) worn by the priest in celebrating Mass, and represents the purple garment in which our Divine Lord was clothed when the rabble, bowing before Him, saluted Him as King of the Jews.

To make amends for the indignity then heaped on her persecuted Founder, the Church endeavors to have this vestment as beautiful and costly as possible, thus showing how the purple robe of scorn and derision has blossomed for us, all radiant with the flowers of paradise ; and it is only at certain seasons that she puts off her shining vesture and dons again the purple garment of penance and mortification.

Liturgical writers tell us that "the large, flowing chasuble was used in the Church until the sixteenth century, but after that period a practice set in of clipping it, first at the shoulders and then down the sides, until it assumed its present shape, which, strange to say, was the work of private individuals rather than any wish or command on the part of the Church."

A modified type of this chasuble is found in the Gothic style which is still occasionally seen.

The stole (which is worn around the neck)

should be about six feet eight inches long and four and a half inches wide,* with fringe two and a half inches deep on the ends. It should have three crosses, one in each end and one in the middle.

The maniple (worn on the left arm) is three feet four inches long. It is made similar to the stole, having in addition ribbons with which it can be fastened to the arm.

The dalmatics, stole, and maniples of the deacon and subdeacon correspond in color and material with the vestments worn by the celebrant, and are similarly ornamented. The dalmatics, however, differ considerably in shape from the chasuble, having square corners, wide, open sleeves, and are trimmed front and back with bands of embroidery.

The stole and maniples are like those of the celebrant, with the exception that the deacon's stole should have two cords and tassels.

VESTMENTS WORN AT VESPERS, BENEDICTION, AND OTHER FUNCTIONS.

The surplice, like the alb, should, according to rubricians, be also of linen, ornamented with narrow lace around the neck, sleeves, and bottom.

---

* Four and a half inches wide across the ends, the middle being not more than two inches wide,

Lace surplices, however, are very generally worn at the present day, at least in this country; while those of fine cambric and lawn, handsomely trimmed with needlework, are sometimes seen. The latter are more in accordance with the rubric, but if made of *linen* cambric would be *still more so.*

Another kind of surplice is made of illusion,* and can be carried in the pocket, which is a great convenience on many occasions. It is neatly trimmed with edging, having often several tucks above the hem.

The dimensions of the surplice as given are: twenty-five inches long, including lace on edge, and eight feet eight inches in circumference; the sleeves seventeen inches long and thirty-two wide; the shoulder-pieces† (edged with lace), four and a quarter inches square. This is a surplice of medium size. The hem on the bottom and sleeves may be five or six inches in width, but if the edge be done in needlework it will need no hem. The neck is gath-

---

* A plain, serviceable lace, sometimes called "wash-illusion."

† Instead of having square pieces set in, the shoulders of surplices are now usually joined together with bands of insertion, the square shoulder-pieces being only seen in the surplices of the sanctuary boys.

ered into a narrow band, with strings of white ribbon for tying it together.

The cope is the large vestment of semicircular form that is worn by the officiating clergyman at Vespers, Benediction, funerals, and in blessing the palms, candles, holy-water, etc. For the latter function it is always of purple, for funerals black, for benediction white or gold, and for Vespers of a color corresponding to the chapter.

The cope is usually of rich cloth, magnificently embroidered in silver and gold, the fronts and cape being often of solid needlework, while the edge is finished with gold or silver fringe.*

The humeral, or Benediction, veil, is the long scarf which the priest wears on his shoulders at Benediction, or when carrying the Blessed Sacrament in procession.

It is of silk, moire-antique, or cloth of gold, with embroidered centre and ends, the latter gold-fringed. It is also bordered around with gold or silver galloon.

Preaching-stoles are considerably larger than those belonging to a set of vestments, and are

---

* In churches where they have cope-bearers, copes of a plainer description are required for them, having the cope simply trimmed with braid and the front bands outlined with two rows of the same,

more elaborately made, being ornamented with embroidery in gold or colored silks, and some-times a combination of both, with rich trim-mings of gold,—cord, tassels, fringe, galloon, etc. They are usually of white or gold cloth. though colored stoles are also used.

Benediction-stoles* are *always* of white, and similar to the preaching-stole. They are worn by the priests when exposing the Blessed Sac-rament.

Confession-stoles † should be as large as the stole belonging to the Mass vestments, and of silk,—purple on one side and white on the other,—thus serving for baptisms as well. They are quite plainly made, having only a cross in the ends and middle of gold, silver, or silk galloon, with a border of the same all around, and fringe on the ends to match, to-gether with cords and tassels or ribbons for fastenings.

For funeral services a black stole is used

---

* Sometimes the priest wears a preaching stole or one belonging to a set of white vestments, but it is proper to have a special stole for each occasion.

† A rubricist, speaking of such stoles, says: "*Confession-stoles* ought to be as large as, or at least not much smaller than, the stole used at Mass. The same must be said of others, except the stole for sick-calls. But those 'minia-ture' stoles to be found sometimes, for confession or bap-tism, are an abomination,"

which can be of silk or velvet more or less ornamented.

A PLEA FOR MORE AND BETTER VESTMENTS.

It is to be regretted that in many churches
otherwise well ordered there is a lamentable
deficiency in the matter of vestments and acces-
sories, thus rendering it impossible to carry out
the ceremonial properly.

The blame generally rests with the members
of the Altar Society, whose duty as well as privilege it is to see that a sufficient supply of vestments be provided to properly equip the requisite number of clergy for the different services and functions.

There are churches, again, where the supply is
ample but the quality *very poor*, the greater part
being of cheap, coarse material, including also
many vestments so *soiled* and *shabby* as to be
totally unfit for a place in the sanctuary.

In the Old Law, only the most precious fabrics—cloth of blue, of scarlet, of purple, and of
fine linen interwoven with pure gold—were
employed in the construction of vestments
worn by the priests in the temple. These
" holy garments " were commanded to be made
" for glory and for beauty." and to be orna-

mented with embroidery interspersed with golden bells, and have also settings of precious stones—emeralds, diamonds, amethyst, topaz, onyx, sapphire, jasper, etc.

As the New Dispensation is not less exacting in regard to *its* holy garments, should we not be zealous in our efforts to equal if not surpass the Jews in the " glory and beauty " of our altars and vestments, especially as we are favored with facilities for having all these things on a scale of magnificence* such as the " chosen people " never so much as dreamed of?

It is because too little attention has been given to the appropriateness of these things which, trifling as they may appear to the uninitiated, play an important part in the sacred functions, that there is such a poor and inadequate supply of vestments in many of our churches.

Where members of a society have leisure to do so, it is a delightful thing to employ it in making vestments, hangings for the sanctuary, etc. We are told that ages ago royal and noble ladies plied their needles for the adorn-

---

* It is not an unusual thing to see vestments nowadays having on them scenes from our Saviour's life beautifully worked in gold and silver embroidery, some of which are perfect marvels of workmanship.

ment of the altar, and that the great St. Dunstan himself did not disdain to design patterns to be executed by their hands.*

It would hardly be fair, however, to expect the ladies to make *all* of the vestments used in the various services. Nor would there be any economy in their so doing, as the embroidery in relief, with which many of the vestments are ornamented, could not be done except by an expert in that kind of needlework (bullion embroidery), and amateurs who have tried the experiment of imitating it declare that a vestment beautifully worked can be purchased for a trifle more than the cost of the bullion with which to do it.†

Silk embroidery, on the contrary, can be very nicely done by many persons, although vestments of the better class are seldom decorated with it alone, gold flowers and emblems being interspersed through it to impart richness.

---

*When the monasteries and convents of England were suppressed at the time of the so-called Reformation, and the nuns could no longer employ themselves in embroidering vestments for the Church, it is recorded that "the ladies of the great Roman Catholic families came to the rescue," among them the widow of the ill-fated Earl of Arundel, "who, with her gentlewomen, was ever busied in work ordained for the service of the Church."

† An inexperienced hand necessarily wastes considerable bullion, which, being very expensive, soon "counts up."

These can be had to set on in certain places, as, for instance, a dove in gold and silver raised work, for a Benediction veil, or gold wheat or grapes, for a stole worked in colored silks, with spaces left for these ornaments.

Or, where ladies cannot do the decorative part and yet would like to have a share in the work, they can procure all kinds of vestments *embroidered but not made up*, to finish which would perhaps be as much as they would care to undertake. They can also find *crosses for chasubles, bands for dalmatics*, and capes and bands for copes, in every style of workmanship, all ready for putting on, together with the necessary trimmings and material for the foundation of such vestments. Put together in this way, they may, in a manner, be considered home-made.

There are, moreover, many other things equally necessary, on which to expend time and ingenuity, such as the linens, hangings, etc.

CARE OF VESTMENTS.

A very important thing in connection with the vestments is to see that they are *properly cared for* when provided.

Once a week all the vestments and laces in every-day use should be looked over, and any necessary mending done, buttons sewed on, and strings, tapes, etc., renewed. Laces, especially if a thread be broken, will soon be beyond repair if not attended to at once. A small break can be easily drawn together; but where there is a large hole, the net might be matched and a piece neatly set in, the ragged edges being cut away. In mending laces, fine embroidery-cotton will be found better than thread.

Vestments do not admit of much repairing beyond putting new galloon on the edges when they begin to look frayed. They are apt to become soiled, however, particularly around the neck, and may be wiped with a cloth moistened with a little household ammonia and water; but if badly greased they must be cleaned with benzine—sparingly used.

Vestments, when not in use, should be carefully put away, each set by itself in a drawer, on which is a label designating the color. The vestments ornamented with raised embroidery in gold or silver should have pads put in between the work, to prevent it becoming flattened or otherwise injured. These pads may be made of white cotton-flannel with a layer or two of batting between. Copes should not be folded up, but put on frames; albs and surplices hung up in wardrobes, stoles put into drawers, and the altar linens and laces likewise put into drawers (each in its own) labelled "altar-cloths," "communion-cloths," etc.; black hangings and draperies in a drawer by themselves, and colored ones the same. All vestments, whether on frames or in drawers, should have a covering over them.

Some Celebrated Vestments.

Among the treasures of ecclesiastical art preserved with great care in churches, museums, and religious houses in the Old World, is a chasuble, which may now be seen in the Castle of Carrouges, France, where it was taken for safe-keeping from a chapel belonging to the castle, before the Revolution. It differs little in shape from chasubles of the present day, and, though regarded as a great treasure, is not at all superior to them in material or workmanship, being, in fact, very like those seen in many of our sanctuaries on almost any Sunday.

"It is made of green brocaded silk, upon which, placed at right angles, are flowers beautifully worked in gold, and blue and white silk bordered with red. The cross, of red silk with silver *fleurs-de-lis*, is much faded by time. Ribands of blue and violet velvet, upon which is written, in Gothic characters, the motto 'Dieu et mon droit,' are arranged so as to form six rings along the upright part of the cross.

Between each of these rings are two crowns, one royal, the other episcopal, placed side by side ; and between them may be observed a large L, sometimes joined to another letter which is too indistinct to be deciphered. These ornaments are richly embroidered in gold. In the centre of each ring is a sun resplendent with gold and silver. It is in strong relief on blue and violet ground, disposed in such a manner as to alternate constantly with the blue and violet of the velvet ribands.

" On the transverse piece of the cross are similar crowns and L's ; and below, placed between the flowers of which we have spoken before, are two shields, gules, *semé* of *fleurs de-lis* argent.

" The front of the chasuble is precisely the same as the back, except that the L's and the crowns are placed horizontally."

There have been many conjectures as to the origin of this curious vestment, which bears the motto belonging to the royal arms of England, " Dieu et mon droit," as well as the shield charged with *fleurs-de-lis*, which would lead one to suppose that it belonged to France. It is thought by some to have been presented by Louis XI. to the chapel of Carrouges when he visited it in the year 1473.

COPE AND MANIPLE OF ST. CUTHBERT.

The rarest specimens of *opus angelicamen** extant are the cope and the maniple of St. Cuthbert, "which were removed from his coffin some years ago, in the Cathedral of Durham, and are now preserved in the Chapter Library of that city; the beauty of the embroidery on which baffles all description. One side of the maniple is of gold lace stitched on, worked, apparently, on a parchment pattern."

A magnificent mitre is also spoken of, which is preserved in the Museum of Rheims. It belonged to the Cardinal of Lorraine, and is said to have been worn by him at the Council of Trent.

" In 1669, the value of the mitre was estimated at 45,000 livres, a sum equal to £2500. The stones were mounted on silver cloth covered with gold filigree, the highest point of the front of the mitre being formed by a figure of St. Michael the Archangel destroying the dragon This was originally ornamented with seventeen small diamonds valued at sixty crowns. A fine turquoise and two rubies, immediately under the image of the saint, were estimated at 400 livres. On the frontal band the title of Jesus, in Gothic letters, was formed of diamonds.

---

* English ' cut or open-work," done in gold.

"Two emeralds engraved, one with an image of the Virgin and the other with an image of the angel Gabriel, were also in the frontal band, which was, besides, decorated with rubies.

"Pearls, emeralds, and rubies formed the edging of the mitre, and exquisite filigree-work was jewelled here and there with precious stones.

"The centre-band of the mitre was peculiarly rich in jewels, and the pendants were formed of cloth of gold."

A RARE ALB.

In the cathedral of Granada there is an alb of rare lace, presented to the church by Ferdinand and Isabella,—one of the few relics of ecclesiastical grandeur* still to be found in that country.

And, coming down to our own times, we read of a lace dress, the most costly work ever executed at Alençon, which was exhibited at the Exposition of 1859, and was purchased by the Emperor of France for the Empress, who afterwards presented it to the Pope as a trimming for his rochet.

---

* Cardinal Wiseman, who had worn this alb, estimated its value at 10,000 crowns.

VESTMENTS IN TAPESTRY-WORK.

The writer was recently shown a very curious and beautiful set of vestments brought from Belgium twenty-five years ago. They were worked on canvas, in tapestry stitch, with colored worsteds and flosses, the design being clusters of roses and leaves richly and artistically shaded.

The stole, maniple, and chalice-cover were of solid work, but the sides of the chasuble were of white brocaded silk, the cross and pillar only being embroidered. The set was lined throughout with red silk and trimmed with gold galloon.

Though they had been in constant wear all these years, the colors were as fresh and unfaded and the work as good as when first executed. There is one objection to such vestments, however; they are very heavy and warm.

ANTEPENDIUMS.

Regarding the antependium, an authority in such matters says, "The *common* opinion of rubricists nowadays is, that where the altar is in *forma sarcophagi* (i.e., where the mensa* is

---

* The table of the altar.

not projected beyond the altar front), and where
the front is nicely worked in carving or sculp-
ture (emblematic), *no* antependium is to be
used for solemn functions; rather during the
week, or on ordinary Sundays or services, such
an ornamented front should be covered with a
plain antependium."

As there are but few altars (comparatively
speaking) in this country in the form of a sarcophagus, it will be seen that the various
antependiums called for by the rubric will be
required in most cases. Where the exception
occurs, however, due attention should be paid
to the instruction given above.

The antependium must correspond with the
vestments in color and richness, and therefore
a full set is necessary in order to have a suitable one for each occasion.

Those of white silk, satin, or cloth of gold,
embroidered more or less elaborately with
silver and gold, are appropriate for the more
solemn festivals, such as Christmas and Easter;
while something of a plainer description, in the
same color (white or gold), will answer for
ordinary feasts, and for Sundays on which
white is used.

Next in importance is a purple antependium
for penitential seasons. This is usually of
silk damask or velveteen with gold or silver

emblem, and trimmed with galloon fringe to match.

A black one,* similarly trimmed, will be required for requiem Masses and funerals. It is forbidden to have on it any emblem of death, such as skull or cross-bones.

Antependiums of red and of green can be of velveteen or silk, handsomely ornamented with silver and gold. In fact, all of the colored antependiums may be made and trimmed alike, together with such of the white ones as are for ordinary days.

Antependiums should be stretched on a frame having hooks or springs at each end, by which it can be fastened to the altar.

In St. Peter's Church (Rome) they are stationary on the altar and arranged in this manner: the antependiums, in five colors, are each affixed to a separate frame of very light wood, all the frames being set in grooves —made for them—in front of the altar, and just back of a broad frame of richly moulded brass which is securely fastened to the altar. This makes a handsome border for the antependiums, any one of which can be brought forward

---

* It is not proper to put a black antependium on the altar of the Blessed Sacrament at *any time*. Therefore such an antependium can only be used in churches having another altar at which requiem or funeral services take place.

by drawing it out of its groove and putting it in front, while the one taken therefrom can be assigned a place in the rear, very much after the manner in which scenery is shifted in a theatre.

Each antependium has a curtain of soft cloth to protect it from contact with the one in front of it.

Members of Altar Societies might easily make some of the antependiums—that is, the plainer ones, which require but little trimming beyond a row of fringe (about a finger deep, running straight across the front eight or ten inches from the top), a few bars of galloon, and an appropriate centre-piece (though the latter is not important on those for every-day use).

Where economy is an object, merino can be used for the black and purple antependiums, instead of silk or velveteen, but it would require an extra heavy lining.

In addition to those enumerated above, it is suggested to have a white antependium, and also one of purple—*not on frames*—which can be used on certain occasions to hang over another antependium when the color has to be changed during the service. For instance, a red antependium is on the altar (that being the color of the office); over this, the white one

spoken of can be quickly hung, where Benedic·
tion of the Blessed Sacrament follows.

ANTEPENDIUMS FOR SIDE ALTARS.

Although specified in the ceremonial of
Bishops, many of our side altars are seen without an antependium. This should not be the
case regarding the altars at which Mass is celebrated, though it is not necessary they should
have a full set of antependiums as for the high
altar; one of white or of gold and one of
purple being sufficient for each altar.

It is allowable to have an antependium of
blue (or of white, embroidered with blue and
gold) on the altar of the Blessed Virgin. It
should have a suitable emblem, or a monogram
in the centre.

One method of making an ordinary antependium is to first stretch tightly over a frame of
the required size the cambric or cloth which
is to serve as a lining, fastening it on with
small tacks at the back. Then cut the material
of which the antependium is to be made into
breadths running lengthwise, which should be
joined together in such a way that the seams
will not pucker (if of merino, they would require pressing, though for small antependiums one breadth of this goods would perhaps

5

answer). Sew on the trimming according to the design wished for, and when finished draw the antependium smoothly over the lining already on the frame, fastening it securely by sewing it to the edges of the lining, or by tacking it to the back of the frame.

CHAPTER V.

Accessories.

Canopies.

THE canopy is one of the most important articles of church paraphernalia, without which it is impossible to have an imposing procession.

There are two kinds of canopy required by the rubric,—the square and the round, the latter called umbrellino, from being umbrella-shaped.

The most elegant canopy made is of white moire-antique, superbly embroidered in real gold, after designs drawn expressly for ecclesiastical needlework, showing symbolic fruits and flowers, with emblematic figures expressive of religious sentiment—a continuation of the sacred imagery on vestments, which forms, as it were, a panorama in art embroidery of the principal events connected with Christianity.

Another style of canopy equally magnificent is of gold cloth, also elaborately embroidered with silver and gold, and, like the one above described, richly mounted and trimmed.

These, of course, are designed for the more solemn festivals; while there are others less costly, but still very handsome, for ordinary occasions. Noteworthy among them is one of white silk interwoven with gold, on which flowers and emblems are embroidered in brilliant colors.

Canopies of red silk, interwoven with silver and gold, are sometimes carried in processions on such days as they are appropriate. They make a pleasing variety; but where only the *required two* can be had, they should be of *white* or *gold*.

The umbrellino* is smaller and more simply made than the canopy proper, although it is usually ornamented with gold figures and emblems, and heavily fringed with gold. It is only used to hold over the priest as he descends from the altar carrying the Blessed Sacrament, to take his place under the square or processional canopy. The umbrellino *must be always of white*.

Like all church goods of the kind, canopies can be procured ready-made, or, if desired, partially made, but in such a shape as to be easily

---

* In Catholic countries the umbrellino is also used in carrying the Blessed Sacrament to the sick and dying.

finished and put together, with all necessary trimmings, viz., lining, fringes, tassels, poles, and knobs.

CANOPY OR VEIL OF THE TABERNACLE.

This canopy* is used in connection with the antependium, with which it should correspond as far as color and material are concerned.

It is made in such a manner as to cover the entire tabernacle, leaving an opening in front so that it can be drawn back on each side in order that the door may be opened when necessary.

Sometimes the canopy is constructed on a frame, thus fitting smoothly over the tabernacle. Again, it is gathered full at the top, and allowed to hang in folds all around.

It can be either embroidered in gold, or only moderately trimmed with gold or silver galloon and fringe.

The rubric does not require a canopy on a tabernacle of marble or stone.

VEIL OF EXPOSITION.

The veil of exposition should be of rich white material, or of cloth of gold, handsomely em-

---

* A black canopy is never allowed on a tabernacle where the Blessed Sacrament is reserved.

broidered in gold and trimmed with fringe and tassels of gold.

It is hung like a banneret, on a standard, and is used during sermons to screen from view the Adorable Sacrament, when exposed on the altar, as it is contrary to the rubric for a con- gregation to sit down in the presence of the Blessed Sacrament unless it is veiled, even to listen to a pious discourse.

To make such a veil a piece of silk about two feet long and a foot and a half wide would be required, together with sufficient gold braid (an inch and a half wide) to border it around, and heavy bullion fringe for the bottom, which is cut in three deep points or scal- lops.

An appropriate emblem in gold can be placed in the centre of the veil instead of embroidery. The veil should be lined with white silk.

The standard may be of gilt or black walnut, with cross and balancing-beam to match.

CIBORIUM-COVERS

are of the same material and color as the above veil, and are likewise ornamented with gold embroidery. Some are simply made of a strip of silk seamed up and gathered at the top, leaving an opening for the cross, which sur- mounts the ciborium, to slip through, while the bottom is edged with fringe. Others are in a circular form, with the opening in front, and others again are in quarters, button-hole-stitched around with twist, inside of which is sometimes a narrow vine worked in silk or gold.

VEILS AND DIADEMS FOR STATUARY.

The custom of having the statue of Our Lady veiled, which has of late years somewhat fallen into disuse, is again revived, and the most beautiful veiling for that purpose is now offered by dealers in church goods.

It comes in patterns of different lengths, and is of tulle, embroidered with gold of a superior quality that will not tarnish or become dis-colored with age. It is of various degrees of richness appropriate to the statue for which it is intended.

Veils of either plain or figured lace are used for ordinary wear, but should be of delicate texture, yet strong enough to bear doing up.

Plain lace having a pattern darned in with linen floss would do nicely for every-day use.

Coarse, heavy lace, such as Nottingham, antique, etc., should not be used for veiling.

DIADEMS.

Diadems (on statuary) are also coming into favor again, and elegant designs, resplendent with sparkling jewels, are shown.

They properly belong with veils, which they serve to hold in place, thus being useful as well as ornamental.

LECTERN HANGINGS

are six feet long, and just wide enough to entirely cover the book-rest. They are sometimes of rich material, and trimmed across both ends with gold braid and fringe; but for Holy Week (when *three* are required) they can be made of merino (purple), and have simply a hem an inch and a half wide all around.

They should be of colors appropriate to different occasions. Black hangings, however, will not be needed, as lecterns are *uncovered* on Good Friday and at requiem Masses and funerals.

COVERS FOR MISSAL-STANDS.

These covers are usually of velvet or heavy brocaded silk, and of colors to correspond with the vestments. They should be large enough to hang four or five inches over the stand, and should be trimmed with gold braid and fringe.

having also tassels at the corners. A centre-piece may be added, and the cover lined with silk or cambric.

The missal may be covered to match the stand-cover, but will need no trimming unless it be a cross of gold braid on the upper side. If at no other time, it would be proper that the missal should have a covering of black or purple on occasions when the vestments are of those colors—especially when the binding is of a bright color.

PULPIT HANGINGS

should be of rich material, and made according to the style of the pulpit on which they are to be placed. They are usually of velvet, plush, or satin-damask, in the form of an upholstered cushion, having drapery edged with heavy silk fringe and ornamented with tassels, though sometimes they are simply hangings of silk, or merino, trimmed with gold braid and fringe. In this case they should be about three quarters of a yard wide, and long enough to extend all around the pulpit.* They may hang straight down, or be festooned. Both styles are seen. Pulpit hangings are generally dark red, except for funerals, when they are black.

---

* Where the pulpit stands in the body of the church, especially in German churches, such hangings are often seen.

ALTAR-COVERS.

An outside covering is necessary for the altar, between the services. This, rubricians say, should be of green cloth or baize, bordered with narrow fringe, and sufficiently large to cover the table and hang over a little all around.

Altar-covers, are, however, to be found nowadays in various colors, handsomely embroidered or plainly trimmed, to suit purchasers; but societies, if disposed, can make their own, in which case it is well to follow the above rule regarding them.

Felt cloth is an excellent substitute for baize; but cheap goods, such as calico or cambric, are unfit for the purpose.

PYX-CASE.

The pyx in which the communion for the sick is carried should have always a covering of white silk richly trimmed. This can be made similar to a burse, but without cardboard, having, in addition, a lapel to fold over the opening; or it may be shaped like a lady's bag, with a handle or cord of white silk which the priest can put around his neck for safe-keeping.

COVERING FOR THE BENCH OF THE SACRED MINISTER.

This covering should be four and a half yards long, and the width of the material of which it is made—said material being baize (or other woollen cloth), green on ordinary occasions, and purple for specified times.

FUNERAL PALL.

For funerals and requiem Masses a pall is absolutely necessary. Like all other church paraphernalia, it may be procured ready-made, of black velvet, merino, or damask, trimmed with silver galloon and bordered with heavy fringe of the same.

Ladies wishing to do so can easily make a pall themselves, but they will not find it any particular saving, unless they make it very plain—say of merino—simply trimmed with silver braid, and lined with cambric.

The pall should be about nine feet long and six in width.

MISSIONARY CASE.

Every church having outlying " missions," or "stations," needs a missionary case which the priest can take with him on his ministrations.

This case when open forms an altar sufficiently large on which to celebrate the sacred mysteries.

When closed it is a handsome mahogany box eighteen inches long, fourteen wide, and about seven in depth, containing everything necessary for saying Mass, viz., a linen and a lace alb, cincture, and amice; linen altar-cloths, with chalice linens and towels; a set of silk vestments—chasuble, stole, maniple, veil of the chalice, and burse, red on one side and white on the other; a chalice, silver cup, and paten, solid silver pyx and oil-stock; one set of cruets, with plates; a silver-plated bell, one wine-flask and bread-box; a brass crucifix, and pair of bracket candlesticks, together with a missal and altar-cards.

It is the most complete thing of the kind to be found, and can be conveniently carried about, occupying but little space, and being easily packed and unpacked.

CHAPTER VI.

Outfits for Acolytes and Sanctuary Boys.

N many churches it devolves on the members of the Altar Society to see that the acolytes are provided with suitable outfits for the sanctuary, and therefore a little information on the subject will not be out of place here.

Where the church ceremonial is fully carried out, two acolytes and six torch-bearers are required to assist at the principal services (High Mass and Vespers). There is no law prescribing how they shall be dressed, but the Christian Brothers have established a rule regarding the color and style of the garments to be worn by sanctuary boys, which has been generally adopted in the larger cities.

The acolytes and torch-bearers are attired in white merino cassocks with red sashes, white lace or muslin surplices, and shoulder-capes of gold cloth trimmed with gold fringe, having also stars of gold in the front and back.

Then there must be two servers, and a master of ceremonies. These are larger boys than the acolytes (especially the master of ceremonies) and wear cassocks of purple merino, white surplices, and purple satin shoulder-capes with gold trimmings, that of the master of ceremonies having in addition the letter M done in gold on the back.

Next come six little boys in white cassocks with blue sashes, white surplices, and blue satin capes; while bringing up the rear are the sanctuary boys, in red cassocks and white surplices.

The surplices are fastened at the neck with bows of ribbon matching the cassocks in color.

All the boys wear white cotton gloves and usually black leather slippers with white stockings.

Generally the parents of the sanctuary boys prefer to furnish these outfits, as in that case each boy can keep his own when his term of office shall have expired as a memento of the time when he was privileged to serve at the altar.

The ladies of the Society, however, would probably have to attend to these outfits being properly made, except in places where there are Christian Brothers to superintend such matters.

Heavy, all-wool merino is considered the best material for cassocks, three yards and a half being required for the larger size and something less for the smaller. From half to three-quarters of a yard of satin for the capes, with gold braid and other necessary trimmings, and the same for the gold cloth capes, together . with a lining of silk or silesia for all.

Three yards and a half to five yards of lace, muslin, or lawn is necessary for a surplice, according to the size of the boy for whom intended. These surplices are usually of the same shape as those worn by the priests (see page 48), but are always of plain (not figured) material, having a hem a finger deep around the bottom and sleeves, above which are five or six tucks, each half an inch deep. A pretty lace, about half an inch wide, on the edge and around the neck, gives a nice finish. The square shoulder-pieces should also be edged with the same lace. Winged surplices without sleeves are occasionally seen in some sanctuaries, but they are never worn in Rome.

The sashes may be of ribbon five or six inches wide.

Barretas are seldom worn, but when they are they should correspond with the color of the cassocks.

"The Sanctuary Boys' Illustrated Manual," by Rev. James A. McCallen, S.S., contains the necessary instruction for such boys.

CHAPTER VII.

How Altar Linens Should be Done Up.

THE members of some Altar Societies consider it a privilege to be allowed to do up with *their own hands* the linens and laces used in connection with the altar, and where such a feeling prevails they are sure to be *done well*.

A very good system, for ladies so disposed, is to take turns in doing them, each one taking entire charge of all the linens for a week or month, as the case may be, and renovating such as are soiled during that time.

When it is not convenient to assume this responsibility, the next best thing is to secure the services of a competent and conscientious woman, who can understand and appreciate the necessity of church linens being differently treated from ordinary linens, and the importance of washing them separately, as it would be a mark of great disrespect to put them in with the soiled linens of her customers.

As there are few laundresses* who would care to take charge of the altar linens subject to such restrictions, the propriety of their being done by the Society will be apparent to all.

In doing up linens and laces, due attention must be given that they are neither too blue nor too yellow, and that they are not starched too stiffly.

Nothing is more painful to the eye than the sight of the priests and acolytes in surplices that are fairly bristling with stiffness, whereas they should fall in soft folds around them.

The lace and muslin surplices require only enough starch to give them a slight dressing, so that they will not hang limp ; but the altar-ruffles should not be starched *at all*, especially where they are of real lace. If carefully washed and ironed while damp they will be found stiff enough for beauty. Altar-ruffles in every-day use require doing up about once a month, while those used only on festivals need not be done more than once a year—say at Christmas, or Easter.

Ruffles, albs, or veils (for statuary) of rich lace will last for years without being washed,

---

* Occasionally a woman may be found who is willing to do the church washing only, in which case it would be safe to intrust it to her.

6

and when necessary should be done by an experienced hand.

When albs require washing, the lace bottom should be ripped off, folded up, and put into a drawer until the linen body is done up, when it can be again sewed on, which, it may be here remarked, is the only *reliable* way of fastening the lace to the body. Hooks and buttons have both been tried and found unreliable, being apt to come undone; of the two, buttons, however, serving the better purpose. It is seldom that the bottom of the alb needs renovating, the body being more liable to become soiled; but even when both parts require washing they cannot be done very well together, but must be separated and each done alone, the result being more satisfactory.

The communion-cloth may be slightly starched, ironed, and rolled up, which leaves it smooth and free from creases; or another way is to iron it in folds about six inches wide, so that when taken from the rails it can be laid in the same folds and put away in a drawer, where it will not get rumpled. The altar-cloths can be treated in the same way.

While it would be very disrespectful to put soiled linen on the altar or allow it to be used in the sanctuary, it is also the duty of a Society to exercise a certain amount of care and economy in regard to unnecessary expenditure* in the renovating and cleansing of it, and, in fact, in everything else that involves a useless out- lay of money ; which money, as a general thing, is the contribution of the poor, who feel an honest pride in giving to the altar, and whose generosity deserves at least the reward of see- ing it wisely and prudently expended.

By saving in such matters societies will be enabled to procure vestments and articles of furniture for the altar that will be both hand- some and lasting.

How often linens should be changed de- pends entirely on how much they are used ; although the following rules, laid down by a rubrician regarding them, will apply to the generality of cases :

" The upper cloth of each altar should be changed once a month, and the under ones four times a year.

" The corporals should be changed after three weeks' use, and the albs, amices, cinctures, and towels when necessary, according to the num ber of clergy.

" The purificators (of which each priest

---

* The laundry bills of some societies are perfectly enor- mous, and, being of constant recurrence, often exceed, at the yearly summing-up, all other expenditures for the altar.

should use his own) may be changed every eight days.

"The surplices in general use should be changed when requisite, the towels of the sacristy every week, the communion-cloth in daily use every fortnight, the larger ones every two months.

"On the greater solemnities, all the linen should be perfectly clean."

Albs and surplices, having been washed, are to be plaited, or at least neatly folded.

Purificators and corporals after use cannot be touched by lay persons, but must be washed by a priest or clerk in Holy Orders, first in hot water, and then in two other waters, after which they can pass into the hands of laics to be done up. The corporal should be well starched and folded in the manner described on page 36.

When perfectly dry the linens should be laid away in their own especial places ; and it is recommended to place with them dried roses, lavender, or other flowers of the kind, for the sake of fragrance and cleanliness as well as to keep insects away.

CHAPTER VIII.

Rules for Cleaning the Altar and Furniture.

VERY day the predella* of the altar at which Mass is celebrated should be swept, or at least lightly brushed.

Once a week the sanctuary should be well swept and the furniture dusted.

The altar and tabernacle require cleaning once a month. If of wood, they may be washed in tepid water, having in it a little spirits of ammonia, which will remove any spots that may be on the paint-work, and will prevent it from turning yellow (if it be white paint).

If there be drippings on the altar from the candles, as is apt to be the case, these should not be scraped off with a knife, but rubbed quickly with a cloth wrung out of hot-water, and they will soon disappear, after which the altar may be wiped dry with a piece of flannel.

Where the altar is of marble, it can be

---

* Platform.

treated in the same manner, and if dim or discolored, powdered pumice-stone—if well rubbed on—will probably remove all stains. A small, stiff brush or a pointed stick will be found useful in cleaning the crevices and carvings, after which the altar may be polished with a soft cloth.

Twice a year the altars should be stripped, the furniture removed from the sanctuary, and the place thoroughly cleaned and left to air until evening, or, if possible, over night, and once a year (at Easter) the carpet will require to be taken up and beaten.

The brass and silver ornaments—candlesticks, crosses, doors of tabernacles, etc.—in daily use should be rubbed every week with a piece of chamois-skin, and, when necessary, washed in soap and water. Ordinary whiting, mixed with water, will remove discolorations from metal. The same treatment will answer for plated ware.

Varnished or lacquered ware, when dimmed from the atmosphere, may be wiped with a moist cloth and rubbed dry with chamois-skin; and gilt woodwork when soiled may be washed in cold water (to which may be added a few drops of ammonia), and wiped dry with a piece of flannel.

Censers, when stained or incrusted with

burnt incense, should be rubbed with sweet oil * and afterwards washed with a brush in hot soap and water, using also whiting if required. Spirits of ammonia will be found excellent for cleaning tarnished brass-ware, imparting also a fine polish. It can be applied with a piece of flannel. A soft brush should be used in cleaning metal-ware having raised work or ornaments.

The sanctuary and other lamps should be cleaned every two weeks, the glass bowls being washed in warm water.

The cruets should be rinsed out every day, and well washed at least once a month. If of metal they will require cleaning oftener.

Articles of metal that are used but seldom need not be cleaned excepting before such festivals where they will be employed in the decorations. In the intervals, however, they should be kept in a dry place, each piece being done up separately in a cotton-flannel bag to prevent tarnishing.

Polishing powders and liquids,† with which the market is now flooded, should not be used

---

* Kerosene oil is said to be excellent for cleaning all kinds of brass-ware.

† Liquids for gilding may perhaps be very good for some purposes, but should never be used on altar furniture in any manner.

for cleaning purposes unless known to be reliable and harmless, as many of them are worthless, serving only to corrode and destroy the metal.

The furniture of the sanctuary—rosewood, black walnut, etc.—when requiring cleaning, can be rubbed with a piece of flannel on which may be poured a few drops of olive-oil, after which it can be polished with a piece of sheet-cork.

This will not be necessary more than twice a year if the furniture is kept covered during the week and dusted every Saturday, and occasionally rubbed with a piece of flannel.

When soiled by handling, wax or sperm candles may be cleaned by wiping them with a piece of flannel moistened with benzine. Refuse scraps of wax and ends of candles should be saved and sent to the factory, where they are made over.

CHAPTER IX.

𝕿𝖍𝖊 𝕾𝖆𝖈𝖗𝖎𝖘𝖙𝖎𝖊𝖘.

THE sacristies should be covered with heavy cocoanut matting, and provided with suitable wardrobes, presses, and closets for holding the vestments and altar furniture.

According to some rubricians, each press ought to have a platform in front of it, about four feet wide and six inches high, as the clergy when vesting should be raised a step from the floor.*

Some of the presses should have shallow drawers, each capable of holding one set of vestments, spread out at full length; but for the linens, laces, and hangings drawers of ordinary size will answer.

It is considered well to have several drawers, lined with cedar, for certain articles, as a precaution against insects, while others might be

---

* When the priest is robing for the altar he stands in front of a press on which his vestments are placed in readiness.

lined with baize, and all in which the vestments are kept have a covering of cambric or silesia to protect them from the dust.

For convenience, every drawer should be distinctly labelled.

Several wire frames, such as clothiers use, will serve well in the wardrobes* on which to put copes; or shoulder forms (only) hung from the ceiling of the wardrobe will answer the purpose just as well, without being so cumbersome as the standing frames.

A small press, having little closets for the chalices, and drawers for the chalice linens, is sometimes placed on the top of a larger press. It is recommended to have small wooden pegs in these closets on which to hang the purificators to dry.

This press also serves as a stand for the crucifix, or for the image of the patron saint of the church, which latter should be in every sacristy.

A large cupboard with folding-doors is necessary for the candlesticks and candelabra, with shelves far enough apart to admit of the large ones occupying the lower section, and the smaller ones the upper, without coming in con-

---

* Wardrobes for sacristies should be large and roomy They are generally made to order, as are also the presses and cupboards.

tact with the wood. A similar cupboard will be wanted for the vases, flower-pots, baskets, and artificial bouquets.

A wardrobe sufficiently large to contain the robes of the sanctuary boys can be placed where most convenient in the sacristy, unless a separate room can be assigned them. Each boy should have a number marked over the peg (or section) his robes are to occupy in the wardrobe, with a corresponding one on his robes, to avoid confusion.

A rack or holder for the acolytes' torches (an iron umbrella-stand is often used) may stand in an out-of-the-way corner. It should have a heavy covering to protect the torches from injury.

One (or more) prie-dieu and confessional combined will be stationary in the priests' sacristy. Over it should be hung the table of prayers before and after Mass, either framed, or mounted on stiff cardboard glazed over.

The Altar Society should have a sacristy to itself, where the ladies could make the necessary preparations without intruding on anybody, or being intruded on or interrupted in their labors. Here they should, as far as possible, have everything they might want to use or over which they are expected to have supervision, so that they need not be obliged to go into the other sacristy, especially when oc-cupied by the clergy.

An indispensable thing in a sacristy is a small sink with water supply, and a table on which flowers can be arranged.

There will also be needed a good supply of brooms, brushes, and feather dusters,* small watering-pots that will be handy for watering plants on the altars and shrines, light wooden pails for cleaning purposes, plenty of good cleaning cloths, both woollen and cotton, with soap, whiting, benzine, and ammonia to be used when necessary. Several tin wash-basins† and dust-pans, and some chamois-skin and soft cloths for polishing, will finish the list of that class of articles which will require a large roomy closet to hold them all.

In this closet may also be kept the censers, holy-water pots, chafing-pan and tongs.

A step ladder that can be easily moved about will likewise be in constant demand, to-gether with two or three small hammers and a supply of nails and tacks.

---

* Several of these dusters might have long handles, en-abling a person to dust the statuary and pictures that are beyond ordinary reach.

† A number of good-sized towels will be required in both sacristies, and they should be *marked*, so as to be known apart.

A work-basket containing a full assortment of thread and sewing silk of colors most likely to be needed, with tape, buttons, needles, scissors, and thimbles of different sizes, should be always at hand, as well as a pincushion well supplied with pins (one should also be left in the priests' sacristy).

In connection with the sacristy should be a place in which the paschal and tenebræ candlesticks, the rod for the triple candle, lecterns, (used only occasionally), and all such things could be put away for safe-keeping.

The sacristies should be kept clean and tidy, no refuse of flowers or waste of any sort being allowed to accumulate, nor things scattered around in a disorderly manner. Articles of furniture or hangings belonging to the sanc tuary should not be left lying loose, but put away in an orderly manner when not in use, both to preserve them and to prevent confusion. Once a year the matting might be taken up from the floor and everything cleaned and thoroughly renovated.

DEPORTMENT IN THE SACRISTY.

It will not be necessary to urge the importance of a quiet, respectful deportment being maintained in the sacristy, as those in charge are generally too well informed on the subject to need any instruction regarding it. There are, however, in every congregation a few idlers who are continually running in and out of the sacristy on the most trifling pretexts, slamming doors and laughing and talking loudly, regardless of the fact that they are in the anteroom of the Holy of Holies, distracting also those who may be in the church preparing for confession or endeavoring to say a prayer.

For the benefit of such persons it is suggested that a piece of cardboard bearing the significant word "Silence" be framed and hung up in a conspicuous place, as is done in some sacristies in Europe; and when these droppers-in—forgetting they are on sacred ground—commence discussing irrelevant subjects, simply point to the *motto*, and perhaps that will sufficiently rebuke them.

On the other hand, it is right to be courteous and civil to those having occasion to come into the sacristy, whether bringing donations of flowers or candles for the altar, or wishing to see the priest on business. If the latter, a little kindly attention in securing them an audience with him will oftentimes be a positive act of charity.

CHAPTER X.

𝕷𝖎𝖌𝖍𝖙𝖘 𝖀𝖘𝖊𝖉 𝖆𝖙 𝖙𝖍𝖊 𝕯𝖎𝖋𝖋𝖊𝖗𝖊𝖓𝖙 𝕾𝖊𝖗𝖛𝖎𝖈𝖊𝖘.

IN specifying the number of lights (candles) required by the rubric for · different occasions, it should be *distinctly understood* that *each candle is expected to be in a separate candlestick,* as it mentions explicitly candlesticks, not merely candles. It is, therefore, contrary to the rubric to light two or more candles on the same candelabrum,* instead of having each candle in its own individual candlestick (see remarks on candlesticks, page 18).

These candles *must be of pure white wax,* with a few exceptions, which will be referred to further on.

AT MASSES.

For Low Mass, two candles, one on each side of the tabernacle.

---

* Although each of the candles specified above must be in a separate candlestick, still at the more solemn functions it is allowable to have on the altar, in addition, candelabra, or branch candlesticks, filled with sperm or paraffine candles. But they should be for ornament alone, and occupy a secondary place

For Low Mass of a public character, such as parochial (community) Masses on Sundays and holydays, four candles.

For a sung Mass (*missa cantata*) without deacon and subdeacon, at least four candles.

For a High Mass (*missa solemnis*), six candles, although more are allowed.

VESPERS AND OTHER PUBLIC DEVOTIONS.

For solemn Vespers, six candles.

For less solemn Vespers, four candles.

For ordinary devotions, two candles.

For Benediction of the Blessed Sacrament, twelve candles.

For the acolytes' candlesticks, two candles, and for the torches, six or eight, according to the solemnity of the occasion.

Four or six special candlesticks with candles of unbleached wax (placed around the catafalque), for the absolution at requiem Masses.

The rubric requiring candles to be of *pure wax* is very exacting, "dispensation from its observance being rarely granted, and then only in extreme cases." Sperm and paraffine candles are strictly prohibited by the Sacred Congregation of Rites;* and it is therefore the duty of those having the altar in charge to see that the law regarding them is not trans-

* The use of gas-lights on the altar is also strictly prohibited.

gressed, as it is fraught with a meaning which is clearly and intelligently explained by a rubrician as follows:

" The only reason why the Church does not admit other than wax-candles is their *symbolism*. This, however, does not merely consist in that the wax typifies the humanity of Christ, and the light (flame) His divinity (for this might be indicated by any other candle); but the *one* reason is that there is no other material to indicate so appropriately the virginal generation of Christ than the production of the bee's fruit. Without being impregnated by the drone, she produces (i.e., brings forth) wax, and honey from the pure flowers. Thus no other material than beeswax is fit to symbolize the immaculate body of the Saviour brought forth by His Virgin Mother.

" A second symbolic reason indicated by the Sacred Congregation of Rites is that wax is rather a representative of the fruits of the earth (vegetable) than of animals. Christ, having by His own bloody sacrifice abolished other bloody sacrifices (of animals), and having instituted under the form of the vegetable order (bread and wine) an unbloody sacrifice, it is appropriate that the candles burnt in holy liturgy— being an offering to God—should be of wax, not of fat (lard or stearine or paraffine).'

7

SPERM AND PARAFFINE CANDLES.*

As will be seen, the rule regarding wax-candles refers to the number actually required in Divine services, such as Mass, Vespers, and Benediction; and therefore sperm or paraffine candles can be used in *addition* to those of wax when a great many are necessary in illuminating the altar.

OLIVE-OIL FOR LAMPS.

Pure olive-oil only must be burnt in the sanctuary lamp, but sperm-oil may be used in taper-lamps for shrines.   Still, olive-oil is preferable, as it burns with a more steady light and is less liable to become extinguished, a point in its favor that will strongly recommend it to any one having the care of such lamps.   It is quite inexpensive, too, costing only one dollar and a half per gallon.

Another very important thing is a good reliable taper for the lamps, one that will burn long enough to pay for the trouble of preparing it.

The unalterable wax-tapers are considered the best in the market by those who have tried all kinds.

---

* Candles improve by being kept some months before using.

CHAPTER XI.

𝔥𝔬𝔴 𝔱𝔬 𝔄𝔯𝔯𝔞𝔫𝔤𝔢 𝔖𝔦𝔡𝔢 𝔄𝔩𝔱𝔞𝔯𝔰.

IN many of our churches the side altars are simply *shrines*, and do not therefore require the furniture necessary for an altar on which the Holy Sacrifice is offered.

They must be provided, however, with a sufficient number of candlesticks, both plain and ornamental, together with such other orments as are appropriate to the character of the shrine, having also each a covering of linen, a lace ruffle, and an antependium if desired.

But where used as altars (even if but occasionally) each one must be furnished with the same number of candlesticks* as the high altar, together with three linen cloths, a lace ruffle, an antependium (corresponding with that of

---

* The Ceremonial of Bishops says: "At *least* two candle sticks with candles of *pure* wax;" but it is customary to have four or six, besides as many others as will contribute to the adornment of the altar.

the high altar), a small missal and stand, a set of small altar-cards, a consecrated stone,† a crucifix, and a bell.

Side altars may be plainly or elaborately decorated, according to their size and general surroundings. If large and handsomely finished they will of course admit of greater ornamentation than those of smaller, simpler make, and may be furnished with rich candelabra, vases of gold, silver, china, etc., for holding flowers and plants, of which there should always be a choice supply.

Where a side altar is the altar of the Blessed Sacrament (so called from the Blessed Sacrament being reserved there), as is sometimes the case in large churches, it " must be adorned," says the rubric, " in a more costly manner than the others," and, unlike them, should have a tabernacle before which a lamp is continually burning.

Altars that are dedicated to the Sacred Heart, Our Blessed Lady, or some of the saints, and having a statue of the same thereon, ought to be decorated in an especial manner on such saints' feast or anniversary, and should at

---

† A consecrated stone covered with linen is necessary in celebrating Mass on an altar which has not been consecrated.

all times as far as possible symbolize the virtues for which they are venerated. This can be easily done by selecting for the adornment of each altar or shrine the flowers designated on page 192 as typical of the various saints in the calendar.

CHAPTER XII.

How to Decorate the Altar and Prepare the Necessary Articles for Mass, Vespers, Benediction, etc.

HIGH MASS ON SUNDAYS AND HOLYDAYS.

THE sanctuary should be thoroughly swept, after which the coverings that have protected the altar and furniture through the week should be removed and everything well dusted.

If the altar is not perfectly clean it may be washed, or at least wiped with a wet cloth, and when dry the crucifix set in the middle (on the tabernacle), with three candlesticks holding wax-candles on each side of it.

As many candelabra as will give a furnished appearance to the altar can be arranged on the steps of it. Between them may be placed reliquaries and flowers, which, however, should never be allowed to conceal in any manner the candlesticks or other furniture of the altar, which *must at all times be the most conspicuous.*

The (three) linen cloths can now be spread on the altar, an antependium of appropriate color put in front, and, where it is customary, a canopy to correspond on the tabernacle,* and a lace ruffle fastened on to the altar-cloths so as to hang over the antependium.

On the Epistle side of the altar will be placed the missal-stand and on it the missal,† open at the Mass, the altar-cards in their respective positions, the larger one in the middle; the Gospel of St. John on the Gospel side and the Ps. Lavabo on the Epistle side. The ablution-cup, about half full of fresh water, must be set on the first step (near the tabernacle) on the right-hand side, with a clean purificator.

It is strictly forbidden to place candlesticks, flowers, or ornaments of any kind on the table of the altar; *nor should they be set on the tabernacle*, or before the door of it.

The credence is to be set in place and cov-

---

* Where the tabernacle is of marble or stone a canopy is not required; and *even when* of wood it may be *dispensed with*, as the following from a rubricist in reference to it will prove: "The outer veil (canopy) when used (its use being free, as the obligation formerly existing is certainly removed by long contrary custom) *must* correspond to the color of the Mass or the office."

† Though not strictly necessary, both missal-stand and missal may be covered with a color to correspond with the Mass.

ered with linen according to directions on page 39, and the following articles* put on it:

The chalice, with purificator, paten, host, and pall, covered with the chalice-veil, on which is placed the burse, containing the corporal.

The cruets of wine and water, with lavabo towel and hand-bell.

The book of the Epistle and Gospel, or a missal, with marks in the right place.

The humeral veil for the subdeacon, which should cover the chalice and hang down on each side of the credence.

The lectern, if used, should have a hanging of a color to correspond with the vestments worn; and where it is customary to have a covering on the minister's bench it must be green or purple, as the case requires.

On the altar in the *sacristy* may be laid the vestments for the celebrant, — the chasuble, maniple, stole, alb, cincture, and amice.

On the right of them the dalmatic, maniple, stole, alb, cincture, and amice for the deacon;

---

* Members of the Altar Society are seldom expected to place the above articles in readiness for the functions, that being the sacristan's duty; but in case they should be, it is unnecessary to remind them that they *must not touch the chalice or any of the sacred vessels* without permission from the bishop, as they are only enumerated here to make the list complete.

and on the left the dalmatic, maniple, alb, cincture, and amice for the subdeacon.

Where most convenient, the surplices for the master of ceremonies and for the three clerks.

The censer and incense-boat, together with fire for the censer, and the processional cross if there should be a procession.

Two candles in candlesticks for the acolytes and the torches for the elevation.

Where the *asperges* takes place before Mass the cope will be laid in readiness in place of the chasuble, the latter, together with three maniples, being placed in the celebrant's seat.

In the sacristy there should also be placed on a credence or stand covered with white linen, the empty holy-water pot and sprinkle; a ritual; some salt in a covered vessel; a jar or vessel of fresh spring water, and a towel; while near by may be laid a purple stole for the priest who is to bless the water, and a surplice and lighted candle for the assistant.

This blessing of the water takes place on every Sunday in the year except Easter and Whitsunday.

A section of the communion-cloth can be left on the railing (provided there is a colored one outside of it) to accommodate those who may receive during Mass; but a better way is to lay it on the credence.

In some churches the piece of linen used for this purpose is about as large as a good-sized napkin.

When Mass is concluded the altar-cards and missal-stand will be removed and the altar-cover spread on, where it can remain during all the other offices or functions *except* Benediction of the Blessed Sacrament.

MISSA CANTATA, OR MASS SUNG WITHOUT DEACON AND SUBDEACON.

The preparations are the same as for High Mass (*missa solemnis*) with the following *exceptions :*

Vestments for the celebrant *alone* will be laid in readiness, the chasuble and maniple on his seat in the sanctuary, and the alb, amice, cincture, and stole in the sacristy.

The censer and incense-boat will not be wanted, nor the candlesticks of the acolytes. The torches for the elevation will be used, however.

The chalice is placed on the altar instead of on the credence.

The cruets will be on the credence as usual, and the Book of the Epistles, the lavabo towel, the communion-cloth, and bell.

The credence will be covered with linen the

same as for *missa solemnis*, and the customary preparations made for the blessing of water.
The lectern will not be required.

LOW MASS.

The altar must be prepared and adorned the same as for High Mass,* with the exception that *four* candlesticks and candles (of pure wax) are required instead of *six*.

The cruets should be placed ready for use on the credence, together with the lavabo towel, and a small communion-cloth in case of priests or acolytes wishing to receive.

In the sacristy, the celebrant's vestments, of the color of the day, should be laid ready for putting on, and two cassocks and surplices for the servers (unless they have another apartment, in which case their robes will be left there).

The communion-cloth should be fastened to the railing, but may be removed after Mass, unless perhaps a section of it be left for the use of those who may communicate at High Mass.

---

* Low Masses on Sundays and holydays of obligation, being public Masses at which the parish people assist, are considered of a different character from the private Masses on week-days. Therefore it is deemed right and proper that the altar should be as well decorated for them as for High Masses.

LOW MASS ON WEEK-DAYS.

Two small candlesticks with candles, on the lowest steps of the altar, one each side, with the crucifix in the middle, the consecrated stone, * three linen cloths and a lace ruffle, the altar-cards and missal-stand having on it the missal closed with the edges turned toward the tabernacle.

The cruets and towels may be put on a small stand instead of on the regular credence; and in cases where clergymen might be obliged to celebrate Mass without a server, the stand can be set on the predella (platform) quite near the altar, or the above articles might be put on the extreme corner of the altar near the Epistle side.

Where Mass is said on a side altar, it should be prepared in the same manner, using, however, the smaller furniture (see page 99).

PREPARATIONS FOR PONTIFICAL MASS

By a Bishop in his Own Diocese.

The altar should present a festive appearance, being adorned in the handsomest manner with flowers and ornaments.

---

* A consecrated stone is only used on altars that have not been consecrated, such as side altars or those in chap els or in places serving as temporary churches.

Three candlesticks with wax-candles on each side of the crucifix, behind which a seventh candle must be placed.*

Besides these, the candelabra, in sufficient number to produce a brilliant effect, can be arranged on the steps of the altar, and between them may be disposed reliquaries and floral decorations.

An antependium of a color corresponding to the vestments should be on the altar front, and canopy to match on the tabernacle.

Pontifical vestments of the proper color should be placed on the altar directly in the middle, one over the other, in the following order: the chasuble, dalmatic, tunic, stole, cincture, alb, and, lastly, amice.

On the Epistle side, near the vestments, the pectoral cross and ring on a silver salver; the golden mitre leaning against the candlesticks, and the crosier at the corner; and on the Gospel side the gloves on a plate or salver, and the precious mitre at the same corner.

The credence on the Epistle side, covered as usual with white linen, and on it the chalice, with purificator, paten, host, pall, and burse

---

* According to the rubric, when a bishop celebrates Mass in his own diocese a wax-candle must be placed behind the crucifix.

containing the corporal. Behind the chalice
the cruets on their plate; the basin and ewer
with water for washing the bishop's hands; two
or three fine towels on a plate; the Book of
Epistles and Gospels; the missal for the bishop,
with his maniple in it, open at the Gospel of the
day; the book called the Canon; the bishop's
sandals and stockings on a plate, covered with
a veil; two candlesticks with candles for the
acolytes, and also a hand-candlestick. Over
the chalice the long veil (humeral) will be
spread, with the ends hanging down on each
side of the table.

The minister's bench, with proper covering,
should be on the Epistle side, below the credence, and against the side wall of the sanctuary. On it the maniples of the deacon and
subdeacon must be placed.

The bishop's seat, or throne, should be on
the Gospel side, against the side wall of the
sanctuary, and on a platform raised three steps
above the floor of the sanctuary, and sufficiently
large to accommodate two wooden stools for
the assistant deacons—on each side of the
bishop's chair—the stools to be without backs
and suitably painted. The bishop's chair, however, should have a high back and comfortable
arms, and be upholstered in silk or satin.
There should also be a third stool, similar to

the others, near that of the assistant deacon, for the assistant priest.

Over the bishop's seat there must be a canopy of graceful proportions, with hangings of rich material on every side, which should be of the color of the vestments worn at the Mass; while the walls back of the chair and stools should have drapery to correspond.

Instead of the usual chairs a sufficient number of benches, having backs covered with drapery, should be placed on each side of the sanctuary for the clergy.

A faldstool, which is used both as a praying-desk and chair by the bishop, will be also in the sanctuary. It must be covered with silk cloth of a color corresponding to the vestments. Two cushions, also covered with the same material, should be prepared, one for the seat and the other to kneel on.

There must be a number of acolytes (no less than eight) in surplices. The first one carries the book, and holds it while the bishop reads out of it (though when he sings the book must be held by the assistant priest). The duty of the second is to hold the hand-candlestick when the bishop reads or sings. The third one, who besides the surplice wears also a cope, carries the crosier. The fourth acolyte, if not dressed in a cope, wears on his surplice a long veil hanging from his neck before him, in order to cover his hands when he holds the mitre. The fifth one is the censer-bearer. The sixth and seventh carry the candlesticks, while the eighth one carries the apron of rich silk cloth that is spread on the bishop's knees when seated.

In the sacristy are to be prepared a cope for the assistant priest; two amices, albs, cinctures, and dalmatics for the two assistant deacons (they do not wear stoles nor maniples); two amices, albs, and cinctures for the deacon and subdeacon; together with a stole for the deacon. Their maniples should be placed on their seats in the sanctuary.

A sufficient number of sacred vestments for the clergy who are to take part in the service, as also of dalmatics and albs for clergymen who are not priests.

The incense-boat and censer should likewise be in readiness here.

In churches that have a side chapel it is required that the pontifical vestments be placed on the altar there instead of on the high-altar.

HIGH MASS FOR THE DEAD.

On the altar there should be six candles of unbleached wax in plain candlesticks, with the crucifix in the centre.

A purple antependium* in front of the altar, and a canopy of the same color on the tabernacle.

The missal, covered with purple, on the missal-stand, open at the Mass for the Dead; the stand to have also a purple covering.

In their places altar-cards of the plainest description.

The credence should be covered with white linen, which must hang but a little over the sides, and on it the chalice should be placed in the centre; the cruets on their stand, with towels on the right; the Book of Epistles on the left, the acolytes' candlesticks with candles of unbleached wax on either side—the candles to be distributed to those in the sanctuary; the communion-cloth if required. (The humeral veil for the sub-deacon will not be needed.)

The celebrant's bench should be uncovered, and the lectern, if used for the Epistle and Gospel, will have no hangings.

The processional cross can stand near the credence.

---

* A recent decree from Rome forbids black draperies or hangings on the altar of the Blessed Sacrament. For this reason at any requiem service taking place there, the antependium and canopy must be purple, unless the Blessed Sacrament be removed from the tabernacle, in which case all may be black.

If there be a funeral discourse or panegyric, the pulpit should be draped in black.

In the sacristy the same vestments as for any High Mass, only of black, should be laid out, together with surplices for the acolytes and servers, the torches for the elevation, the acolytes' candlesticks, the censer and incense-boat, with fire and tongs ; and, if absolution is given after Mass, a black cope for the celebrant, a ritual, and the holy-water pot and sprinkle.

A catafalque can be arranged in the usual place and surrounded with lights.

LOW MASS FOR THE DEAD.

The altar can be prepared the same as for High Mass, with the exception that only two candlesticks are required.

Vestments for the celebrant alone should be in readiness in the sacristy.

FORTY HOURS' ADORATION.

For this solemnity the altar should be richly adorned, the most costly ornaments and rarest exotics being employed in beautifying the throne of the Blessed Sacrament.

The place of exposition in the upper tabernacle (or on a portable throne) will have a corporal spread over it, and be surrounded with flowers, lights, and blossoming plants,

According to the rubric, " no statues or relics of saints are allowed on the altar (with the exception of the figures of the adoring angels, which may be permitted to remain). If there be a picture over the altar, it, and the walls near it, must be covered with rich drapery, representing, however, nothing profane." *

The antependium must be always of white (or cloth of gold), even though the Mass requires a different color.

The altar-cards and missal-stand will be on for the Mass,† together with six candlesticks with wax-candles, and six additional ones to be lighted at the exposition, thus making the *twelve wax-candles* required to be kept burning during it.

Besides these, sperm and paraffine candles can be arranged on the steps of the altar to enhance the radiance.

On the credence, which is to be prepared in the accustomed manner, should be placed the necessary articles for High Mass, and also the monstrance covered with a white veil, the host fastened in the crescent, the book containing the litany and other prayers, a cope of the color of the vestments for the celebrant, and

---

* This refers to cloth representing historical subjects or having on it figures of animals or objects foreign to religion.

† After which they will be removed from the altar.

a white stole for the priest who is to expose the Blessed Sacrament.

In the sacristy the usual vestments of appropriate color may be prepared for the celebrant, deacon, and subdeacon, also the processional cross, two censers and incense-boats, the processional canopy and umbrellino, two books with the litany for the chanters, and a sufficient number of candles for the procession.

A bench * covered with cloth or carpet can be placed in the sanctuary for the clergy who remain at the adoration. On it may be several white stoles for the priests who will come at various times to adore.

A lamp should burn before the tabernacle of the side or other altar where the Blessed Sacrament is reserved. It would be fitting to have four wax-candles also lighted here during the time of the exposition, as is the custom at Rome.

On the second day of the exposition, Mass *Pro Pace* is celebrated at the altar where the Blessed Sacrament is reserved; therefore it must be made ready for the function. The other preparations are the same as for Solemn Mass.

---

* A number of kneeling-desks will do instead of a bench, if more convenient.

Purple vestments are worn at the Mass *Pro Pace*.

For the Mass of Deposition, on the third and last day, the same articles will be prepared in the sacristy and on the credence as for that of the first day, with the exception of the host in its crescent, and the monstrance. The high-altar will be prepared the same as for Solemn Mass.

During the exposition, the flowers and lights* will need replenishing from time to time, and the same care and vigilance recommended in connection with the repository must be exercised to avoid accidents by fire, etc.

SOLEMN VESPERS.

The altar may be as profusely decorated with lights, plants, and flowers as good taste will allow, the flowers being arranged in bouquets, baskets, etc.

They should be placed on the steps, but *never on the table of the altar*, as it is contrary to the rubric to use it as a flower or candle-stand ; and, aside from this natural objection,

---

*The admonition against placing flowers too close be-side or above the lights cannot be uttered too often. They quickly become dried from the heat of the candles, and in that state easily ignite.

there is still another argument against it, viz., that it is impossible to properly incense the altar if thus obstructed.

As before stated, it is also forbidden to set flowers or other ornaments on the tabernacle, or before the door of it, at any time.

The linen coverings and lace ruffle are to be on the altar the same as for Mass, together with an antependium of the color corresponding to the Vespers, and a canopy on the tabernacle to match (if desired).

The altar-cards and missal-stand must be removed.

The crucifix will be in the centre, having three candlesticks, with candles of pure wax on each side.*

Reliquaries may be placed between the candlesticks, unless Benediction of the Blessed Sacrament should follow, in which case (as they would have to be removed) they need not be put on.

A lectern with hangings of the color of the vestments to be worn will be placed in front of

---

* Six wax-candles *only* are required for Vespers; but where Benediction is given at the close, twelve at least are requisite, and therefore that number of candles should be put on the altar when preparing it for Vespers, together with as many of sperm or paraffine as will properly illuminate the altar.

the celebrant's chair, which ought to be covered with green or purple, as the Vespers require.

Also a stool for the master of ceremonies near the celebrant's seat, and stools or benches on each side (in front of the altar) for the cope-bearers, which benches are also to be covered with green or purple.

IN THE SACRISTY.

A surplus and cope of the color of the chapter will be in readiness for the celebrant; and if Benediction is to follow, a stole of the same color.

Two or four copes of corresponding color for the cope-bearers, together with the same number of surplices; also four surplices for the master of ceremonies and servers.

Two candlesticks with candles for the acolytes, and the censer and incense-boat.

Where Benediction of the Blessed Sacrament is given immediately after Vespers, without the celebrant leaving the sanctuary, as is the custom in most of our churches, a white humeral veil will be left on the credence or in some convenient place, which he will put on over the cope he wore during Vespers, and the antependium and canopy of the tabernacle will not be changed, even if of a color other than white.

But if at the close of the Vespers the celebrant withdraws from the sanctuary, then *all*
will be changed to white for the Benediction,
and six additional candles lighted.

SOLEMN PONTIFICAL VESPERS
By a Bishop in his Own Diocese.

The altar should be beautifully adorned with
lights, flowers, and other ornaments, the same
as for Solemn Vespers.

The table of the altar is to be covered with
a long veil,* which should hang down on both
sides, but not in front.

In the middle of the altar are to be placed
the sacred vestments of the bishop—the amice,
alb, cincture, stole, and cope. On the Epistle
side the ornamented mitre, and on the Gospel
side the golden mitre; on the highest step near
the Epistle corner the crosier; and near the
vestments on the Gospel side the pectoral cross,
and the ring on a small plate.

On the credence the two candlesticks for the
acolytes, the hand-candlestick, and the missal
for the prayers to be sung by the bishop.

In the centre of the sanctuary two or four
stools for the cope-bearers, according to their
number.

---

* Humeral veil.

In the sacristy must be prepared a cope for the assistant priest ; two amices, albs, cinctures, dalmatics and stoles for the assistant deacons, two or four copes for the chanters, and a sufficient number of copes, chasubles, dalmatics, amices, albs, cinctures, and surplices for the clergy who may assist at Vespers; the censer with incense-boat, and a chafing-pan with fire and tongs.

VESPERS FOR THE DEAD ON THE FIRST DAY OF NOVEMBER.

The purple antependium* on the altar *under one of white*, and a canopy of the same color on the tabernacle, *also under a white one.*

On the credence a black cope for the cele brant, and in a convenient place the lectern with white hangings.

In the body of the church a catafalque covered with a funeral pall, and surrounded with candlesticks (six) holding candles of unbleached wax.

The white ornaments will be removed from the altar at the close of the Vespers, together with the flowers and reliquaries, and likewise the white hanging from the lectern, which will now remain uncovered.

---

* If the Blessed Sacrament be not in the tabernacle the antependium and canopy will be black.

BENEDICTION OF THE BLESSED SACRAMENT.

The preparations for Benediction alone, as laid down in the Roman Ceremonial, are as follows :

There should be at least twelve lighted candles on the altar whenever the Blessed Sacrament is exposed in the monstrance and Benediction given with it.

Likewise a throne or small canopy * should be placed on the highest step over the altar, between the candlesticks, and in it a corporal or pall on which the Blessed Sacrament is to be placed.

On the altar a burse with another corporal, the monstrance covered with a white veil, and the key of the tabernacle.

On the credence a white humeral veil and the book containing the prayers.

In the sacristy a surplice, white stole, and cope for the officiating priest.

A surplice and white stole for the priest or deacon who is to expose the Blessed Sacrament ; and, if there are sacred ministers, two white dalmatics, a white stole for the deacon, two cinctures, two albs, and two amices.

A sufficient number of surplices for the clerks

---

* The *Thabor*, or *Exposition*, is intended for this purpose.

who are to assist the priests, and for the torch-bearers, together with two, four, or even eight torches.

BENEDICTION AFTER MASS.

Where Benediction is given immediately after Mass, the celebrant keeps on the stole he then wore , but, having taken off the chasuble at his usual seat, he puts on a cope of the color used at Mass.

If High Mass be celebrated with deacon and subdeacon, they take off their maniples and assist at the Benediction.   Twelve candles will be lighted the same as for Benediction follow-ing Vespers.

BENEDICTION WITH THE CIBORIUM.

The altar may be more plainly adorned than for Solemn Benediction, six candles being suffi-cient, although a greater number may be lighted. On it should be placed the burse containing a corporal and the key of the tabernacle, and on the credence the book of prayers and a white humeral veil.

A surplice and white stole for the celebrant, and surplices for the servers, together with the censer and incense-boat.

CHAPTER XIII.

Sacraments and Funerals.

SOLEMN BAPTISM.

SURPLICE and purple stole may be laid out in the sacristy for the priest who is to administer the sacrament, together with a surplice for his assistant; the *Rituale Romanum*, a vessel of salt, and the baptismal register, with pens and ink.

At the font the Holy Chrism and oil of catechumens, with some cotton on a plate; the baptismal water in the font, and a shell to pour it on the head of the person to be baptized, together with a basin to receive the water, and a soft linen towel to wipe the head; a white stole and a piece of linen to represent the white garment; a lighted candle, some crumbs of bread on a plate, and water and towels for the priest's hands.

When the ceremony is concluded, the water which was poured on the head of the person baptized, the crumbs of bread, and the water in which the priest washed his hands are to be put into the piscina, while the cotton used in the ceremony must be burnt, and the ashes also put in the piscina.

CONFIRMATION.

The altar to be tastefully adorned with flowers and ornaments, having also six candles lighted.

On the credence a vessel containing the Holy Chrism, a white plate with a quantity of cotton divided into small pieces, the Pontifical book, a hand-candlestick with candle, some thin slices of bread (without any crust) on another small plate, a ewer and basin in which the bishop can wash his hands, and still another plate holding clean towels.

On the altar the bishop's vestments, the amice, stole, cope, mitre, and crosier, arranged in order.

A throne for the bishop will be erected on the Gospel side of the sanctuary, with canopy and hangings of royal purple,* and the fald-

---

* Royal purple is the proper color for the hangings on the bishop's throne, except when he celebrates Mass, when they must be of the color of the day. That particular shade of purple being difficult to obtain, however, dark crimson is often used instead, it having a purplish tinge, and being preferable to violet, which is the penitential color, and therefore *unsuitable*. For directions how to erect the throne, see page 110.

stool will have white hangings and white cushions.

In the sacristy surplices should be prepared for the assistants, and a book of registration, with pens and ink.

Four boys, dressed after the manner of those who attend at High Mass, may be in readiness, one to hold the crosier, another the mitre, another the book, and the fourth the hand-candlestick.

In some churches it is customary to place benches outside the sanctuary railing on which the candidates for confirmation can be seated. This would only answer where the candidates were few in number. The better way is to seat them in the front pews.

Two good-sized candles of wax might be prettily trimmed with white flowers, and tied around with white satin ribbon into graceful bows and ends. These are to be carried by the attendants of the candidate who is to read the vows.

A very suitable decoration for this occasion would be a banner bearing the episcopal arms of the diocese, placed in the sanctuary, or the episcopal arms, formed of flowers, and fastened to the wall at the side of the bishop's throne.

FIRST COMMUNION.

The altar may be handsomely decorated as for confirmation, and the usual articles and vestments for Mass prepared, together with two trimmed candles to be used at the renewal of the "baptismal vows."

If the baptismal font is in the church, it also might be decorated with flowers and trailing vines, and any other feature of adornment introduced which would be consistent with the rubric and appropriate to the event, as these "red-letter days" in children's lives should not be lightly passed over.

THE MARRIAGE SERVICE.

For the performing of the marriage ceremony, a surplice and white stole for the priest who is to officiate may be prepared in the sacristy.

Also a surplice for the server, the holy-water pot and sprinkle, the ritual, a small tray on which to place the ring to be blessed, and a register, with pens and ink.

The altar, if desired, can be adorned with lights and flowers.

If the ceremony takes place with a nuptial Mass, the contracting parties may be furnished with kneeling-stools in front of the altar, but outside the sanctuary railing. In this case the holy-water pot and sprinkle can be left on the credence, as it will not be wanted till the Mass is nearly ended.

CHURCHING OF WOMEN.

A surplice and white stole for the priest, and a surplice for the server should be prepared in the sacristy, together with the ritual, holy-water pot, and sprinkle.

A sufficient number of candles must also be in readiness, which are to be given lighted to the persons who are to be churched.

FUNERALS.

At funerals where there is no Mass—the burial service only being read—the black antependium* can be on the altar and candles of unbleached wax, but nothing more is needed.

In the middle aisle the catafalque or bier covered with a black pall, and surrounded with four or six requiem candlesticks furnished with unbleached candles; and if a sermon be preached the pulpit must have black hangings.

In the sacristy the holy-water pot and sprinkle should be prepared, together with the processional cross, a surplice, black stole, and cope

---

* If the Blessed Sacrament be kept in the tabernacle, *no black* must be on the altar.

for the clergyman; surplices with black rib-bon-bows for the servers, and the acolytes' can-dlesticks furnished with unbleached candles.

At the funerals of children under seven years of age the altar is in white and the candles are all white, and the cross, if carried, is without its staff.

The priest is robed in a surplice and white stole, and the servers wear white bows to fasten their surplices.

According to the Sacred Congregation of Rites, but one cross should be carried at a funeral, even where the clergy and religious societies of several parishes assist at the obse-quies. The cross of the parish to which the de-ceased belonged should only be used.

Side altars are not dressed in black at Masses for the dead or at funerals, unless the services take place at them.

No flowers or ornaments (save the candle-sticks) are placed on the high-altar on such oc-casions; and, although there is no law prohibit-ing it, the custom of taking floral emblems from the casket at the close of a requiem ser-vice, and putting them on the high-altar, is strongly condemned by rubricians.

It is very fitting, however, to place them on the shrine of Our Lady as an offering for the departed soul.

When occasion arises, the church may be draped in mourning, taste being exercised in the material used as well as in its arrangement. A lavish display of cheap goods is anything but a mark of respect to either living or dead. Velvet or woollen fabric is the only thing suitable for such hangings.

CHAPTER XIV.

𝔥𝔬𝔩𝔶 𝔖𝔢𝔞𝔰𝔬𝔫𝔰.

𝔄𝔯𝔱𝔦𝔠𝔩𝔢 𝔉𝔦𝔯𝔰𝔱—𝔄𝔡𝔳𝔢𝔫𝔱.

SUNDAYS IN ADVENT.

INSTRUCTIONS laid down by rubricians regarding the preparing of the altars for Sundays in Advent are that they may "be adorned in a partially festive manner" with flowers, relics, etc., placed between the candlesticks, on the third Sunday (Gaudete Sunday), on which occasion the deacon and subdeacon wear dalmatics.

On all the other Sundays the altars are to be devoid of ornament, having only six candlesticks of the plainest description,* with the crucifix in the centre, and the purple antependium in place. Purple vestments are worn, with folded chasubles† for the deacon and subdeacon.

---

* When plain candlesticks cannot be had, those of brass or gilt may be covered with purple cloth, and unbleached candles used, if possible.

† A folded chasuble is made by folding up the front of an ordinary purple chasuble until it reaches a little above the

When, however, the vigil of Christmas happens to fall on the fourth Sunday, the same order of things prevails as on the third Sunday.

Article Second—Lent.

ASH WEDNESDAY.

The altar should be plainly dressed without flowers, plants, or other decorations.

On it must be placed six candlesticks, with the crucifix in the centre.

The purple antependium in front, and the altar cards and missal-stand in proper position.

On the Epistle side the vessel containing the blessed ashes, covered with a small purple veil (or its own cover will answer).

On the credence the articles necessary for High Mass, together with a plate with crumbs of bread, a ewer of water, with basin and towel, and the holy-water pot and sprinkle.

Close at hand the censer and incense-boat, together with a chafing-dish and fire.

A purple chasuble and maniple for the celebrant will be laid on the minister's bench, and two maniples for the deacon and subdeacon.

waist, where it is held in place with hooks and eyes; or pins will answer, if securely put in. It is generally turned up on the outside. In Rome, such chasubles are usually made short in front, instead of being folded up.

In the sacristy the purple cope and stole, with alb, amice, and cincture for the celebrant ; and stole of the same color, with amice, alb, and cincture for the deacon ; and the same articles, with the exception of the stole, for on the subdeacon.

SUNDAYS IN LENT.

On Sundays in Lent the altars are dressed the same as in Advent, the only difference being that they are partially adorned on the fourth Sunday (Lætare Sunday) instead of on the third one.

On the evening before Passion Sunday all images, pictures, and crosses in the church must be covered with purple. This includes the crosses on the stations also.

Article Third—Holy Week.

PRELIMINARY PREPARATIONS.

There is a great responsibility resting on the members of an Altar Society in connection with the ceremonies of Holy Week, as on them depends the preparing of many things essential to its proper observance. If the work, however, is systematized, it will be more easily and quickly done.

It is an excellent idea to have all the candlesticks, candelabra, gold and silver vases, and other metal ornaments (that are not in use during Lent) washed and polished the week be fore, so as to be in readiness when wanted.

Then *a few good workers*—together with some young members who are anxious to be instructed in this important work—might commence preparations on Monday morning in Holy Week.*

Where it is possible to do so the sanctuary carpet should be taken up, and not put down again until Holy Saturday, thus leaving the sanctuary bare during the solemn offices of the week, as it should be, strictly speaking.

The furniture should all be removed from the sanctuary, which should be well swept, any dust or cobwebs that may have gathered on the walls or around the statuary being also brushed away. The high and side altars should then be stripped (the priest having first, if he thinks proper, removed the Blessed Sacrament from the tabernacle) and thoroughly washed and cleaned. (See page 85.) As it will probably be necessary, in doing so, to kneel on the table of the altar in order to reach to the steps and around the tabernacle, a piece of cloth may be

---

* It is important to have the sacristy in which the preparations are made well warmed, as at this season churches are usually cold and damp.

first spread over the table. When the altars are dried and aired, altar-cloths of the plainest description may be put on the high-altar, together with two plain candlesticks (and candles), the crucifix, altar-cards, missal, and missal-stand.

If, however, the ordinary Masses of the week should be said at a side altar, then that altar should be dressed as above, instead of the high-altar, which may be left uncovered, to air, for several days.

The celebrant's seat and other sanctuary furniture can be cleaned after the manner described on page 88.

There are two advantages to be derived from getting this work done early in the week.

Firstly, the society can have possession of the sanctuary then, there being no services after the morning Mass on Monday until Wednesday; and, secondly, it will be a great relief to have that *important* part over, so that it will not interfere with the preparations that must be made later on.

On Wednesday morning the Tenebræ candlestick can be brought out, wiped, and filled with unbleached candles. If such are not to be had, white ones may be colored or painted with gamboge. Candles of the same kind will also be put inot a plain candlestick for the altar, which is to be otherwise prepared as directed on page 143.

In Europe, where the floor of the sanctuary and the steps and platform of the altar are of marble or stone, the ordinary carpet is taken up, and one of purple put in its place during Holy Week, except on Good Friday, when the altar is to be entirely bare.

A breadth of purple merino two yards long, and hemmed around, will do as a substitute for such a carpet. Quite a number of confession-stoles should be in readiness for clergymen who may come to assist in the confessional.

The principal work of the day, however, is the preparing the repository (see page 145), and for this purpose it is necessary that the ladies should have a room to themselves, free from intrusion, where they can arrange the flowers, plants, lights, and other decorations.

To facilitate matters, one person might take charge of the candlesticks and candles, getting them in readiness to put on the altar. One or two others might arrange the flowers and attend to the plants, seeing that the pots are suitably covered ;* while the rest will have all they can do in preparing the hangings and

---

* Plant-pots, unless ornamental, may be covered with gold or silver paper.

draperies of silk, satin, and lace, sewing on gold braid, fringe, and spangles where needed, and otherwise employing themselves.

As much as possible should be done toward preparing the repository before the congregation assemble for the Tenebræ, as it is very embarrassing to be climbing up and down the altar, and passing in and out the sanctuary, when there are people in the church. If everything be made ready for the decorations beforehand, it will not take long to arrange them on the altar when the services are over ; and, in fact, it would be much better if the flowers were not put on until morning, as they can be kept much fresher in a cool place. They would need to be arranged the night before, however.

The high-altar will also have to be prepared for Holy Thursday with clean linens and laces, and with flowers * and lights. As flowers enter largely into the decorations of Holy Thursday and Easter Sunday, it is important to take some steps toward securing a sufficiency of them beforehand, especially as other denominations have commenced trimming their

---

* The choicest flowers should be reserved for the repository, and some fragrant buds and blossoms will be wanted to strew before the Blessed Sacrament in the procession. They may be placed loosely in small white baskets having handles by which they can be carried.

churches profusely for the latter festival, there-by increasing the demand for exotics of every description.

The customary way in cities is to order a fair supply of flowers some weeks ahead from the florist, and have also a notice read in church on Palm Sunday, soliciting donations of lights and flowers for the repository and for Easter (or the money with which to procure them).

There are, besides, many persons who will send flowers if personally appealed to, who would not otherwise think of doing so. A member of the Society should be delegated to receive such contributions when they are brought into the sacristy, and put them in water, that they may not wither by lying around.

It is likewise well to take the names of parties bringing such contributions, that credit may be given where due.

The large and small canopies can be brought out the last thing Wednesday evening, when there will be room in the sacristy to set them in place. If they have been taken apart they can then be put together, and left in readiness for the morning, with a covering over them to protect them from the dust. The processional cross, covered with a square of purple merino, should also be ready.

The principal duties of Holy Thursday consist in replenishing the candles on the repository, and having a general supervision over
everything.

The high-altar will also have to be prepared
for the Tenebræ, and when that office is ended
the black hangings put up for Good Friday; the
cross on the altar must be covered with black, as
well as a larger crucifix to expose for veneration, the covering on the latter being put on in
such a manner as to be easily removed.

It is recommended to spread the veil bias-
wise over the figure, drawing the corners of it
around to the back of the cross and pinning
them neatly in place with large black-headed
pins, fastening it first at the feet, then at the
left arm, then at the right one, and lastly at
the head, care being taken that the heads of
the pins are in sight, so that the priest may
have no difficulty in uncovering it. The stationary cross on the altar must also be covered
with black.*

Three purple cushions must be in readiness
for the prostrations. They are usually about
thirty inches long and twenty wide, and can be
of merino or any woollen goods, and made

---

* Veils, hangings, and coverings for pictures and statuary
should be of woollen material.

after the manner of a sofa-pillow. Both sides should be of woollen or velvet, as if lined with cambric or silesia they would be liable to slip when in use. Common moss, such as can be procured at an upholsterer's, will do to stuff them with. A fourth cushion (made the same), on which the crucifix can rest during the Veneration, will also be wanted.

If the repository is taken down on Good Friday, the hangings, laces, etc., used in its construction should be folded up at once and put away where they belong. The plants must be watered and set where they will not be too warm; and if there are any flowers, which can be kept over for Easter, they may be put in a cool place for preservation.

The candlesticks, which will probably be covered with drippings of wax, will require cleaning, as well as the altar. *

The high-altar must again be made ready for the Tenebræ, and the many things necessary for the functions of Holy Saturday prepared, as given in detail further on in this chapter.

On Holy Saturday there is much to be done in getting ready for Easter, and the work should be commenced as early in the day as possible, in order that it may be satisfactorily accomplished. The sanctuary of course will have to be swept and dusted and the altar cleaned again before it can be adorned for the great festival of the morrow.

These preliminary preparations pertain only to such work as may be done beforehand and to such things as will be required in the preparations proper for Holy Week, each day of which is given as follows, according to the Roman Ceremonial :

PALM SUNDAY.

The altar should be unadorned, having on it six candlesticks only, of the *plainest kind*, the crucifix, altar-cards, missal, and stand, the purple antependium, and on the pulpit a covering of purple.

In churches where it is customary, branches of palm may be placed in vases between the candlesticks.

On the Gospel side of the sanctuary three lecterns with purple hangings should be placed for the Passion.

On the Epistle side, near the altar, a small table covered with white linen may be prepared for the palms, and a purple veil laid on it, to be used as a covering for the palms.

The processional cross, covered with a purple veil,* in a convenient place, together with a

---

* A purple ribbon should be fastened to the top of the processional cross, with which to fasten a sprig of the palm after the blessing.

chafing-pan, with fire and tongs; the censer with incense-boat.

ON THE CREDENCE.

The chalice covered with the veil.

The missal for the Epistle and Gospel, and a large purple stole for the deacon; a pitcher of water, with basin and towel.

The cruets on their plate, the holy-water pot and sprinkle.

On the celebrant's chair a purple chasuble and maniple, in which he will be robed before beginning Mass.

IN THE SACRISTY.

The purple cope and stole, amice, alb, and cincture for the celebrant; a folded chasuble, stole, and maniple of purple, and amice, alb, and cincture, for the deacon ; a purple folded chasuble and maniple, together with an amice, alb, and cincture, for the subdeacon.

Three amices, albs, and cinctures, three purple stoles and maniples, and three books for the deacons who sing the Passion.

When the bishop blesses the palms the credence containing them will be placed between the altar and his throne. The episcopal vestments will be laid in proper order on the altar, and those of the assistants where convenient ; the book, gremial, bugia, silver plate for the zucchetto, faldstool with cushions, ewer of water, basin, and towel in suitable places.

TENEBRÆ OFFICES.

For the Tenebræ services, which occur on Wednesday, Thursday, and Friday, the altar should be stripped of everything, except the linen cloths, and six plain candlesticks, with candles of unbleached wax, three on each side of the cross.

A purple antependium on the front of the altar, and a purple carpet on the platform.

The triangular candlestick with fifteen unbleached candles placed on the floor of the sanctuary, at the Epistle side, and an extinguisher put near at hand; also an uncovered lectern in the middle of the sanctuary, for the lessons.

The antependium, however, should only be on the altar for the first Tenebræ office—that of Wednesday. On the two succeeding evenings the altar will be *denuded of it and the linen cloths*, leaving on *only* the cross and six candlesticks with candles of unbleached wax.

The other altars in the church will be dressed, or rather undressed, in the same way, except the one where the repository is prepared.

HOLY THURSDAY.

The high-altar is to be handsomely adorned as for a great festival, having on the candelabra and large candlesticks filled with white candles; the crucifix in the centre, covered with white; a white antependium, and a canopy of the same color on the tabernacle.

The credence covered with white linen, and on it the usual articles for Mass, and, in addition, a chalice for the repository, with pall, paten, and a white veil with ribbon of the same color. On the paten used at Mass two hosts, a pyx, with small hosts, white stoles for the priests who are to communicate, a white cope for the celebrant, and a wooden clapper (to be used instead of a bell).

The canopy, umbrellino, and processional cross—the latter covered with a purple veil—in the most convenient place.

In the sacristy, the richest white vestments should be laid in readiness, together with two purple stoles to be worn at the denuding of the altars; an amice, alb, cincture, and white tunic for the cross-bearer, the acolytes' candlesticks, six or eight torches for the elevation, two censers with incense-boats, and a sufficient supply of candles for the procession.

On the side altars (with the exception of the

one used for the repository) the antependiums and coverings of crosses should be purple.

THE REPOSITORY.

The repository is separate and distinct from the altar at which High Mass is celebrated, being usually at a side altar, or in a chapel. It should be beautifully adorned with choice flowers, tastefully arranged in baskets and bouquets, with rich blossoming plants, and with innumerable lights. (Of the latter, *six at least* must be candles of pure wax.)

The urn or tabernacle in which the Blessed Sacrament reposes may be covered with a canopy of white silk, satin, velvet, or cloth of gold, which can be either cut and sewed into shape, or draped over the tabernacle in a graceful manner.

It may be handsomely trimmed with gold embroidery and fringe, or galloon and fringe alone would be sufficient ornamentation, and, if perfectly plain, would serve very well.

When the tabernacle is covered a corporal will be placed in it.

An altar-stone is not necessary on the repository, and only *one* altar-cloth is required ; but the altar-ruffle should be on, and also a white or gold antipendium.

Hangings and draperies of lace and silk are

sometimes a feature in repository decorations ; but great care must be exercised, as a breath of wind may waft them too near the lights, causing them to take fire. For this reason they are not recommended.

Where the treasury of the Society will admit of the expenditure, rare and costly fabrics and ornaments should be used in adorning the repository, but otherwise it is in better taste to employ only flowers and lights, which of themselves are a very suitable decoration and far more in keeping with the spirit of the rubrics than a display of cheap finery could possibly be.

A semicircular range of small steps, painted white, with gilded edges, placed at the back of the altar is in some cases useful in holding candlesticks and plants, thus forming a solid background. A better way, however, is to set the large gold candlesticks (belonging to the high-altar) as far back on the steps of the altar as possible, placing between them tall calla lilies.

On the table of the altar candelabra and smaller candlesticks (with candles) can be disposed in order, interspersed with flowers, which latter must not be placed too near the lights, otherwise they will wither, and even take fire. Where there are large baskets or forms of flowers, they may be set on ornamental stands on the platform of the altar, in front of the repository, or at each side of it,

Some of the flowers will perhaps have to be replaced by fresh ones if the repository stands until Holy Saturday (as it does in some churches), and the plants will require watering.

A corporal and burse should be laid on the altar, together with the key of the tabernacle.

On each side of the repository kneeling-desks may be placed for the use of the clergy, and conveniently near to it steps on which the priest can stand to reach to the tabernacle when necessary.

A taper lamp should burn continually before the repository, the Sacred Heart lamp being most suitable for the purpose. It is the custom now in churches where there are a sufficient number of sanctuary boys, to have them watch in turn—half an hour at a time—at the repository, to attend to the lights, and also to serve as a guard of honor. If possible, two should go on duty at once, occupying the kneeling-desks at either side of the altar. Members of the Altar Society should also have an allotted time each to stay in the church or sacristy and see that everything is properly attended to, and in case there are not boys enough, they themselves must do the watching.

As an extinguisher will be constantly needed, one may be left standing in a convenient place.

A plate or box is usually set at the foot of the altar in which worshippers may deposit their offerings to be used in defraying the ex-penses of the repository. In some churches the collection on Holy Thursday is also appro-priated to this purpose.

GOOD FRIDAY.

The altar should be entirely bare, with the exception of six candlesticks (of the plainest description*) with candles of *unbleached wax.*

The crucifix covered with a black veil in such a manner that it may be easily removed (see page 139).

Three purple cushions† placed on the edge of the platform of the altar, one in the middle and one on each side, at a little distance apart.

The credence covered with plain linen hang-ing only a little over the sides and without a ruffling of lace.

On it should be placed the missal on its stand for the celebrant, another missal without a stand for the ministers, a lavabo, an altar-card, a large black stole for the deacon, a

---

* The golden candlesticks are taken from the altar of St. Peter's Church in Rome during this season and wooden ones put in their place.

† Directions as to size, etc., of these cushions will be found in the preceding chapter,

folded altar-cloth large enough to cover the altar without hanging down.

A small vessel with water, and a purificator in case the priest should need it.

A black burse containing a corporal, and a purificator laid on it ; a black veil for the chalice; the cruets on their plate.

Two candlesticks with unbleached candles for the acolytes, and the wooden clapper.

On the Epistle side of the sanctuary a pur ple carpet ;* a purple cushion large enough for the crucifix, which is to be exposed for veneration, to rest on, and a long white veil ; also three uncovered lecterns for the Passion.

The processional cross, veiled with purple, in any convenient place.

The pulpit must be *uncovered*, and also the minister's bench (chair), no hangings of any *color* being allowed on either of them on Good Friday.

In the sacristy the black vestments should be laid out in the usual order, a chasuble for the celebrant, two folded chasubles for the deacon and sub-deacon, three maniples, two stoles, three albs, amices, and cinctures.

Besides these, three other albs, amices, and cinctures, and the same number of black man-

---

* A strip of purple merino will do.

iples and stoles, and three missals, for the deacons who are to sing the Passion.

A chafing-pan with fire and tongs, two censers and incense-boats, together with the candles and torches for the procession.

HOLY SATURDAY.

The altar is to be dressed in white and adorned as for a solemn festival.

A white antependium on the altar and a white canopy on the tabernacle, with purple ones over them, which are to be removed before Mass begins.

The cross should be in place in the centre of the altar, and the gilt or brass candlesticks and candelabra, furnished with white candles, can be ready for the sacristan or acolytes, to set on the altar when the purple is removed, together with the flowers,* reliquaries, and other ornaments.

On the Gospel side of the sanctuary, the Paschal candlestick, with the candle lying across it, all prepared for lighting, and having in it five holes in the form of a cross for the grains of incense. Also a stand for the triple candle.

If there be a pulpit the *Exultet* will be sung

---

* Artificial flowers will serve very well, reserving the natural ones for Easter.

in it, and therefore it must have a white cushion or drapery, but where there is none a lectern with white hanging should be set out on
the Gospel side. On the Epistle side there
should be an *uncovered* lectern for the Prophecies. The sanctuary and other lamps, ready to
light, may be at hand.

IN THE SACRISTY.

A purple cope and stole, an alb, amice, and
cincture for the celebrant should be laid ready
to put on; together with two folded chasubles
of the same color, two maniples, and a stole, two
albs, amices, and cinctures for the ministers.

Close at hand, if not under the same, may
be laid the usual white vestments for the
celebrant, deacon, and subdeacon; the holy-
water pot and sprinkle; the censer, with incense-boat, a plate with five large grains of
incense, the candlesticks with white candles for
the acolytes, and the processional cross.

The baptismal font should be thoroughly
cleaned and scoured. Any water that is in it
ought to be emptied into the piscina. A table
is to be placed beside or near it, covered with
a linen cloth which need not hang over the
sides more than a quarter of a yard or so. On
it are placed a ewer of water and a basin, a towel
on a plate, a slice of bread (cut moderately
thin, without any crust, and divided into small

squares), with some slices of lemon on a plate ; some clean white cotton also on a plate, the empty holy-water pot, and the sprinkle.

The vessels containing the oil of the cate-chumens and the sacred chrism are likewise to be on the table, but the clergymen generally attend to them. If it is the custom to dis-tribute to the faithful the water blessed on this day, one or more barrels should be pre-pared for it, by covering them with white cot-ton cloth, and trimming them with smilax, myrtle, or ivy, twined in long wreaths and fas-tened around the top and middle of the barrels with pins.

A dipper and tunnel will be found useful in filling up bottles which are brought by parties wishing the water.

In the porch—or, if it be too small (as is often the case). in the next best place—there should be a table covered with white linen in the man-ner described for the one at the baptismal font, on which will be laid a white dalmatic, stole, and maniple for the deacon , a purple maniple for the sub-deacon ; a missal, and a plate con-taining a small candle with matches to light it.

Near the table a chafing-pan with dry pieces of wood, which will be easily lighted from a flint, and beside it tongs with which to put the new fire into the censer : also the triple candle on its rod, decorated with flowers or vines at the part where the stock of the candle connects with the rod.

EASTER SUNDAY.

The altar should be richly and profusely adorned with flowers, lights, and ornaments.

The candlesticks and candelabra filled with white candles, a white antependium on the altar, a white canopy on the tabernacle, and a white hanging on the lectern.

The credence, prepared in the customary manner, having on it the necessary articles for High Mass; and in the sacristy the vestments of white or gold, with albs, amices, and cinctures, for the celebrant and assistants, placed in readiness, together with the censer and incense-boat.

The acolytes' candles may be trimmed with myrtle or smilax.

Conspicuous among the decorations should be the calla or Easter lily.

Perhaps the following description of an altar adorned for the festival may furnish a few suggestions:

" The altar was a revelation of beauty, even to those accustomed to seeing it in festive attire. The pure white marble reflected the gleam of countless lights, and formed an admirable background for the rare and beautiful flowers which were arranged upon it in every conceivable shape and form. Rich tropical plants blossomed in niche and corner, and high above all stately lilies reared their heads proclaiming the 'Resurrection.' The side altars were profusely decorated, and in every available place in the sanctuary gilded stands were seen bearing elegant baskets of fragrant flowers."

Preparations for the Ceremonies of Holy Week, including Ash Wednesday,

FOR CHURCHES WHERE THERE IS BUT ONE PRIEST.

In accordance with the Small Ritual of Benedict XIII., S.M.

ASH WEDNESDAY.

ON THE ALTAR.

The cross, and candlesticks with candles, but no flowers.

The purple antependium and missal on its stand.

A vessel containing the blessed ashes, with a cover the same as the vessel, or else having a purple veil spread over it, and placed between the missal and the Epistle side.

ON THE CREDENCE, NEAR THE ALTAR.

A chalice with a purple veil.

A purple chasuble and maniple.

The holy-water pot and sprinkle.

The censer and incense-boat.

A plate with crumbs of bread, and a basin and pitcher of water to wash the priest's hands after distributing the ashes.

A towel, and a plate containing the cruets, with wine and water, and another small towel to wipe the fingers.

IN THE SACRISTY.

Three surplices for the acolytes.

The alb, amice, cincture, and purple stole and cope.

A chafing-dish, with fire and tongs.

PALM SUNDAY.

ON THE ALTAR.

The purple antependium.

Six candlesticks and candles, with branches of palm between.

The missal on its stand, and the altar-cards.

ON THE CREDENCE.

The chalice, with its ornaments* of purple for Mass.

---

* By ornaments are meant the chalice-veil and burse.

The chasuble and maniple, of purple.

A basin, with pitcher of water and a towel.

The censer and incense-boat.

The cruets, containing wine and water, and a finger-towel.

Copies of the ceremonial for what is to be recited.

ON THE FLOOR OF THE SANCTUARY AT THE EPISTLE SIDE.

A table, covered with a white linen cloth, and on it the palms to be blessed.

The processional cross, covered with a purple veil.

IN THE SACRISTY.

The alb, amice, cincture, and purple cope and stole for the celebrant.

Three surplices for the acolytes.

A chafing-dish, with fire and tongs.

The holy-water pot and sprinkle.

Things to be prepared for the Tenebræ offices are the same as those in churches where there are three or more priests, which will be found under that head, page 143.

MAUNDY (OR HOLY) THURSDAY.

The altar is adorned as for a solemn festival, the front veil (antependium) being white.

The cross between the candlesticks is to be covered with a veil of white.

The missal to be placed on a white cushion or book-stand.

ON THE CREDENCE.

The chalice for Mass, with white ornaments. Another chalice, with a pall, paten, white veil, and a white silk ribbon.

A pyx, with small particles to be consecrated for the communion of the people.

A small plate, with the wine and water cruets, a towel for wiping the fingers, and a wooden clapper.

The processional cross, covered with a purple veil.

A censer, with incense-boat.

A white veil for the priest's shoulders.

The communion-cloth.

The canopy for the procession.

IN THE SACRISTY.

Surplices for the clerks.

The alb, amice, cincture, maniple, stole, and chasuble, all of white.

A white cope and stole.

A chafing-pan, with fire.

Candles for the procession.

The repository to be arranged similar to directions and suggestions given on page 145.

GOOD FRIDAY.

The altar is to be altogether bare, having on it six plain candlesticks with unbleached candles, not lighted.

A crucifix, covered with a black veil put on in such a manner as to be easily removed. (See page 139.)

A black cushion on the second step of the altar.

ON THE CREDENCE.

A linen cloth covering the table without hanging down.

An altar-cloth folded, and large enough to cover the altar without hanging down.

A black burse, containing a corporal, pall, and purificator.

A book-stand with a missal.

The censer, with box containing incense.

A black veil for the chalice, to be used at the end of the office.

A little plate with the cruets and finger-towel.

NEAR THE TABLE.

A carpet and cushion of purple, and a white veil adorned with golden and purple silk fringe.

The processional cross covered with a purple veil.

The wooden clapper.

AT THE REPOSITORY.

Three surplices for the acolytes.

The amice, alb, cincture, black maniple, stole, and chasuble.

A chafing-dish with fire and tongs.

HOLY SATURDAY.

OUTSIDE THE DOOR OF THE CHURCH.

A table covered with a white cloth, and on it :

A small book-stand and missal.

The censer with the box containing incense.

The holy-water pot and sprinkle.

A plate with five grains of incense.

A white maniple, stole, and dalmatic.

A lantern with a candle and flint.

Also, near the table, a chafing-dish—with coals or wood to be lighted for the new fire—and tongs.

A long ornamented rod with the triple candle fastened on the top. This has but one common stock from which three candles rise.

AT THE HIGH-ALTAR.

The altar is to have on the candlesticks and cross, as for a solemn festival.

Its front is to be covered with two antependiums, a white one under another of purple.

A stand on the Gospel side in which to fix the rod with the triple candle.

On the same side a lectern for the *Exultet*, with white hangings.

The Paschal candle, on a large candlestick, the wick of which should be so prepared as to light easily, and five holes in the form of a cross to be made in it for the grains of incense.

The lamps of the church prepared at proper and convenient places.

ON THE CREDENCE.

The white linen covering.

A missal for the *Exultet* and for Mass.

The chalice covered with a white burse and veil.

The cruets with wine and water, and a small linen towel.

IN THE SACRISTY.

The amice, alb, cincture, with purple stole and cope, also a purple maniple, stole, and chasuble.

A white maniple, stole, and chasuble.

A white veil.

Four surplices for the acolytes.

Candles to accompany the ciborium when the priest brings it back to the altar.

AT THE BAPTISMAL FONT.

A table covered with white linen hanging but a little over the top.

Two towels.

The holy-water pot and sprinkle.

Vessels to fill with water from the font.

The vessels containing the oil of the catechumens and holy chrism.

A pitcher of water with basin for washing the hands, and a few slices of bread without crust, on a small plate, with some slices of lemon, for the same purpose.

Some clean cotton on a plate for wiping the fingers.

If baptism is to be administered, add likewise:

The Roman Ritual.

A small plate with salt.

A white stole and cope.

A towel to wipe the head of the baptized person.

Another piece of linen for the white garment.

A candle to be lighted.

11

CHAPTER XV.

𝔉𝔢𝔰𝔱𝔦𝔟𝔞𝔩𝔰.

CHRISTMAS.

F all the festivals in the year Christmas is the one on which Catholics take pride in adorning their altars and churches in the most elaborate manner, to do honor to the " new-born King."

The first of December is none too soon to engage the evergreens for trimmings, and, about two weeks before Christmas, the ladies of the Society should meet in the sacristy, or an adjoining room, each afternoon or evening, to tie the wreaths, a great many yards of which are necessary to make even a moderate display.

It is customary for the sanctuary boys to assist in the work—stripping the boughs and keeping the ladies supplied with sprays of the requisite size for making the wreaths. This facilitates the work to a great degree.

When the wreaths and garlands are all finished, the services of two or more men will be required in getting them put up throughout the church, on walls, pillars, etc.*

The manner of trimming a church with greenery is so well known that a description would be superfluous, though it may not be amiss to state that ornamented shields and bannerets† are nowadays employed in Christmas decorations, as well as the old-time illuminated texts.

The altar is to be prepared and adorned as for any great festival with flowers and innumerable lights. A white canopy on the tabernacle and a white antependium on the altar-front; while rich vestments of the same color, and according to the number of the clergy, may be laid in readiness in the usual place.

The candles of the acolytes should be wreathed with greens, and the lectern hung with white.

---

*Several hammers, together with wire, twine, nails, and everything necessary, should be at hand, so there need be no delay in getting the trimmings up in good season, as it makes so much confusion when done at the last moment, and in haste.

†For information regarding them, as also for *wreaths, floral devices,* and other decorations, see chapter on Church Decorations, page 180. Where parties cannot make the wreaths for want of time or material they can procure them ready made in all the larger cities, where a great variety is to be found each year for Christmas decorations. In some churches the young people of the congregation unite in tying wreaths, thus relieving the Altar Society of much labor.

An ablution cup and an extrá purificator will be provided for each priest for the midnight and other Masses. They may be placed on the credence, which is to be prepared in the accustomed manner.

Where the Divine Office is sung before and after the midnight Mass, the following articles should be in readiness: For Matins (before Mass), a lectern with a book open at the lesson. On the credence a white or gold cope and the acolytes' candles. Seats in the usual places for the cantors, and near them the white copes they will put on at the ninth lesson. For the Lauds, the white or gold cope for the celebrant, placed on the credence during Mass. The lectern with white hangings, on the Epistle side (out of the way), and the reed with tapers and extinguishers, also the censer and incense-boat.

The crowning glory of Christmas decorations is a handsome crib, generally placed near the altar, or in a side-chapel.

This beautiful devotion was instituted by St. Francis of Assisi in 1223, and has continued with undiminished fervor in many localities o Europe down to the present time. In this country, when seen at all, the crib has, until recently, been a miniature affair, chiefly intended to interest and instruct children in the wonderful mystery of the Incarnation.

But the crib* of to-day is something quite different, being a beautiful and life-like representation of the stable of Bethlehem, showing the crib containing the divine Infant, with His Virgin Mother and St. Joseph bending over Him ; while grouped around are the shepherds —crooks in hands—the three kings, kneeling in adoration before the manger, the angel who brought the glad tidings, and, high above all, the Christmas star is shining.

The whole thing is artistically arranged, and calculated to charm the eye as well as to excite devotion in the hearts of both old and young.

FEAST OF THE PURIFICATION.

The altar should be prepared as usual, having on altar-cloths, ruffle, six candlesticks with wax-candles, and the crucifix in the middle ; a white antependium in front, with a purple one over it.

A small table covered with linen must be placed near the altar on the Epistle side, and on it the candles to be blessed, covered over with a white linen cloth.

On the credence, the cruets, holy-water pot and sprinkle, chalice, ewer with water, basin and towel, plate with crumbs of bread, stole for the deacon, and books for the procession.

---

*See catalogue of church goods.

A white humeral veil to be spread over the credence, and outside of it a purple one, which, like the purple antependium, will be removed before Mass begins.

A white canopy can likewise be on the tabernacle under one of purple.

The processional cross in its customary place, together with the censer, incense-boat, and a chafing-dish, with fire and tongs.

On the celebrant's seat a white chasuble, stole, and maniple. On the deacon's, a white dalmatic, stole, and maniple, and on that of the subdeacon a white dalmatic and maniple.

If, however, the Mass should not be of the Blessed Virgin, but of Septuagesima or Sexagesima, the vestments will be of purple instead of white.

In the sacristy the vestments worn at the blessing of the candles will be in readiness, viz., a purple cope, stole, cincture, alb, and amice for the celebrant; a folded chasuble and stole of purple, with cincture, alb, and amice, for the deacon; and a folded chasuble of the same color, with cincture, alb, and amice, for the subdeacon.

Some of the blessed candles should be reserved in the sacristy to be distributed afterwards to those who are unable to be present at the ceremony, but are desirous of obtaining one or more of them. Many persons bring candles with the understanding that they are to receive a certain number back when blessed. Those having them in charge should therefore mark such packages when brought, so that there may be no mistake in regard to the matter.

It should be borne in mind that the candles to be blessed should be of pure wax, and not of sperm or paraffine.

In churches where there are not sacred ministers, the vestments for the deacon and subdeacon, together with the humeral veil, need not be prepared.

Unless the Mass should happen to be of Septuagesima or Sexagesima, the sacristan will (while the procession is in progress) remove the purple antependium from the altar, the canopy from the tabernacle, the cover of the same color from the minister's bench, placing green on it instead, and the purple veil from the credence.

He should also take away the table on which the candles were placed for the blessing; and if there are flowers, previously prepared, set them in place between the candlesticks on the altar.

Where there are but few candles to be blessed, they can be laid on the altar instead of being put on a table.

THE VIGIL OF PENTECOST.

On the vigil of Pentecost baptismal water is usually blessed in churches where they have fonts, for which the following preparation must be made :

The altar is to have a purple antependium, and a purple canopy on the tabernacle, over red ones, besides the other things necessary for the Mass, such as candlesticks, altar-cards, etc.

An uncovered lectern and Book for the Prophecies may be placed in the middle of the sanctuary, and the seat of the sacred ministers covered with purple over green.

On the credence, the usual articles for Mass, together with the Paschal candle, a purple cope for the benediction of the font, and a red burse, over which must be spread first a red and over that again a purple humeral veil.

In the sacristy, the vestments for the opening ceremonies, viz., purple chasuble, stole, and maniple, alb, amice, and cincture for the celebrant; purple folded chasuble, stole, maniple, alb, amice, and cincture for the deacon; purple folded chasuble and maniple, alb, amice, and cincture for the subdeacon. In another place a complete set of red vestments for the Mass, as also the acolytes' candles, censer, and incense-boat. When, towards the close of the Litanies, the celebrant and his assistants withdraw to vest for Mass, the purple antependium and canopy can be removed from the altar, the flowers placed thereon, and the candles lighted.

CORPUS CHRISTI.

If the procession should take place after Mass, besides the usual things necessary for High Mass, the following will be required :

On the credence, a white cope for the celebrant, the monstrance covered with a white veil, the Host in its crescent, and the *Processionale Romanum*, together with candles for distribution.

On the altar, which should be otherwise handsomely decorated, twelve candles of pure wax, a white antependium, and a canopy of the same color on the tabernacle. There must, however, be *no relics* or *images of saints* on the altar.

If there be an Exposition, a clean corporal will be spread on the throne above the tabernacle, and a white stole will be needed for the priest who is to expose the Blessed Sacrament.

In the sacristy, rich white vestments will be laid for the celebrant and assistants, the acolytes' candles, two censers and incense-boats, six or eight torches, the large and small canopy, the processional cross, and, if the procession passes out of the church, four lanterns containing candles.

In churches where it is the custom to strew flowers before the Blessed Sacrament, *these* also may be left in the sacristy, arranged in suitable baskets. If, however, the procession should occur after Vespers, the following preparations will be made:

The altar will be decorated as for any Solemn Vespers, the antependium and tabernacle veil (canopy) being white; the flowers and lights tastefully arranged, twelve of the latter being candles of pure wax; a corporal, monstrance, and the key of the tabernacle.

On the credence a white humeral veil, and missal containing the prayers of the Blessed Sacrament.

In the sacristy a white cope, stole, alb, amice, and cincture for the officiant; a dalmatic, stole, alb, amice, and cincture for the deacon; a dalmatic, alb, amice, and cincture for the subdeacon; with the customary vestments for such other priests as may participate. Also the processional cross, the acolytes' candles, the large and small processional canopies, one or two censers, with boats, and four lanterns with candles.

Where the procession is in the open air, the streets or way through which it is to pass should, if possible, be decorated in a becoming manner. If of sufficient length, small altars may be erected at certain distances, and adorned with lights and flowers, but *no cross.*

Benediction is not given but once or twice during the procession.

The corporal is generally carried in a burse by a clerk.

ALL SAINTS' DAY.

The altar will be appropriately adorned, having ornaments—antependium, veil of tabernacle, etc.—of white or gold.

Vestments of the same color prepared as usual, together with the other articles necessary for the service.

ALL SOULS' DAY.

The church will be draped in mourning (where it is customary), and a catafalque erected in the middle aisle, surrounded with candles of unbleached wax.

The altar plainly dressed, and without black drapery, that is, if it *be the altar of the Blessed Sacrament;* if *not,* it may be hung in black also.

Black vestments will be in readiness according to the number of clergy, and everything prepared as for a requiem Mass. (See page 112.)

FEAST OF THE PATRON SAINT.

The altar is to be dressed and adorned in the manner usual for High Mass, the color being that of the office.

In the sacristy, vestments, etc., are to be in readiness according to the number of clergy assisting at the service.

FEAST OF THE DEDICATION OF THE CHURCH.

The same preparations will be made as for the feast of the patron saint; and should either of the feasts occur in Passion week, the crosses and images in the church should remain covered, in which case the altars will be only partially adorned.

Lights are to be burned before the consecration crosses on the walls, during the sacred offices, on the anniversary of the church dedication.*

OTHER FESTIVALS.

On festivals not specially referred to here, such as the Immaculate Conception, Epiphany, Annunciation, Assumption, etc, the preparations necessary for their proper observance are

---

* It would likewise be appropriate on both the above feasts to have the church, as well as the altar, decorated in a tasteful manner.

very nearly the same in each case as for those given.

Preparations for lesser feasts differ from these mainly in regard to the color of vestments etc., to be worn.

Below are the colors assigned to different days :

White, on the festivals of the Blessed Trinity, Our Lord, and also on all feasts of our Blessed Lady, and of the Saints, martyrs excepted.

Red, on Pentecost, Invention of the Cross, and feasts of the Apostles and Martyrs.

Purple, in Advent, Lent, Ember-days, and Vigils.

Green, on Sundays when there is no special feast occurring.

Black, on Good Friday, and for Masses for the Dead.

CHAPTER XVI.

Month of May.

THE beautiful custom of decorating the shrine of Our Blessed Lady in an especial manner during the month dedicated to her honor, dates back to early Catholic times, when her devoted children of every age and condition brought offerings to lay at her feet while they implored her help and intercession.

Where the shrine of the Blessed Virgin is also an altar, Mass is said there on week-days during May, as well as the other services appropriate to the month, which take place morning and evening. The altar will, therefore, have to be prepared each day (Sunday excepted) for a Low Mass, according to instructions for side altars on page 99.

In addition, flowers, plants, and lights can be arranged on the altar in such a manner as to leave the table clear until Mass is over, when they may be tastefully disposed around. Among the plants particularly appropriate to such shrines is the calla lily, which is typical of purity as well as being of beautiful and stately appearance.

It is not advisable to have a large display of common plants on steps or stands each side of the altar, nor in front of it. They are often an obstruction when the devotions take place, and, besides, the atmosphere of most churches is not favorable to the growth of plants in general, which require light and warmth, otherwise they become sickly and faded.

The draperies and other decorations should be of as rich a description as possible, yet in good taste. The veil of the statue, in particular, should be of a superior quality of lace, as from time immemorial only the most exquisite laces were deemed worthy to adorn the image of the Queen of Heaven.

" Of so great value," says Beckford, speaking on this subject, " were the laces of their favorite Madonnas, that in 1787 the Marchioness of Cogalhuds, wife of the eldest of the semi-royal race of Medina-Cœli, was appointed Mistress of the Robes of Our Lady of La Solidad at Madrid, an office much coveted by the nobility."

The crown that is worn on the statue on ordinary occasions should be taken off and replaced with a handsome diadem reserved for such seasons.

It is the custom, in many churches in Europe, to have a candle-stand near the shrine, in which those disposed can place lighted candles as votive offerings. These are capable of holding ten or twelve candles. Something similar is recommended here, as many of the faithful would gladly avail themselves of the privilege of making a votive offering of candles to the shrine, one of which they could set lighted in the stand while their petition went up to the Mother of Christ for a favor for themselves or for those who were dear to them. These little practices are a great incentive to devotion and should be encouraged.

In congregations where there is a sodality of the Children of Mary, it is a fitting thing to invite them to assist in taking charge of the shrine during the month; and where they are qualified to assume the entire care of it, that would be still more appropriate.

Every day the flowers and plants will require fresh water, the former being replaced, when withered, with others. The candles will also need replenishing daily, and the dried leaves that have accumulated on the altar brushed off, and any drippings of wax from the candles cleaned away.

CHAPTER XVII.

𝔥𝔬𝔴 𝔱𝔬 𝔒𝔯𝔤𝔞𝔫𝔦𝔷𝔢 𝔞𝔫 𝔄𝔩𝔱𝔞𝔯 𝔖𝔬𝔠𝔦𝔢𝔱𝔶; 𝔱𝔬𝔤𝔢𝔱𝔥𝔢𝔯 𝔴𝔦𝔱𝔥 𝔅𝔲𝔩𝔢𝔰 𝔞𝔫𝔡 𝔅𝔢𝔤𝔲𝔩𝔞𝔱𝔦𝔬𝔫𝔰 𝔱𝔥𝔢𝔯𝔢𝔣𝔬𝔯.

 GOOD plan for organizing an Altar Society in a new parish is for those interested in the matter to have a notice read from the altar inviting the ladies of the congregation to meet in the church after High Mass or Vespers, for the purpose of forming such a society.

When assembled, the meeting might be called to order by the pastor, or some one authorized by him, who, after explaining the object and benefits of such a society, would propose for office, the names of candidates selected with a view to requisite qualifications.

The following rules—few in number, but practical in spirit—adapted from one of the most successful societies in the United States, may be of some assistance in perfecting the organization,

12

RULES AND REGULATIONS OF ST.* ———'S
ALTAR SOCIETY.

The society to have four officers—a president, vice-president, secretary, and treasurer.

The duties of the president are to preside at the meetings of the society, and have a general supervision over everything connected with the sanctuary, seeing that each member conscientiously performs the duties assigned her, and that any work given out by the society is likewise done in a satisfactory manner.

She should also endeavor, by example as well as by precept, to inspire her associates with an appreciation of the importance of carrying out the rubrics, even in the smallest detail, for which purpose it will be necessary to thoroughly inform herself regarding them.

The vice-president to act in the absence of the president.

The secretary will take charge of the books of the society, recording the names of members and keeping a strict account of all money received as dues or contributions, and from whom; together with that paid out, and to whom, for necessary expenses — a detailed statement of which will be prepared and read at each annual or semiannual meeting.

---

* Add name of patron saint.

She will also write announcements of meeting, and notices for monthly Masses for living and dead members of the society.

The treasurer shall have charge of the funds of the society, paying therefrom all bills presented—after they have been audited by the president.

The first Sunday of each month a meeting will take place, at which time such members as were on duty the month previous will retire in favor of those appointed to take their places during the coming month,—two or three members serving in this capacity together, who will be expected to leave everything in a good condition when their term of office expires.

An annual election of officers will occur on the first Sunday in January, the candidates to be put in by vote of the society.

Any person may become a member of the society by paying a yearly due of one dollar, or a monthly due of ten cents, the members being divided into two classes — active and honorary—sharing equally in the benefits of monthly Masses said for the society ; the active members being entitled, in addition, to a requiem Mass at death.

Members of the society are also expected to attend the funerals of deceased members, whether active or honorary.

CHAPTER XVIII.

𝔊𝔥𝔲𝔯𝔠𝔥 𝔇𝔢𝔠𝔬𝔯𝔞𝔱𝔦𝔬𝔫𝔰.

HE beauty of church decorations depends entirely on their appropriateness. Considerable taste and a good deal of *common-sense* must therefore be exercised both in the design and execution thereof, remembering that a twofold object is to be attained, viz., beautifying the house of God, and at the same time conveying to the minds of the people, by sign, symbol, and coloring, the sentiments that animate our holy Church in thus celebrating her festivals with pomp and ceremony, in which lights, flowers, garlands, and hangings play an important part.

So much has already been said in these pages regarding the ornamentation of the altar, that further reference to it is unnecessary, save to remind the reader that tawdry, meaningless, or profane devices should never be placed thereon (or indeed allowed anywhere within the church). A simple bouquet of flowers, a plant, or a bough of green is far more beautiful and in keeping with the rubrics than many of the floral designs (horseshoes, etc.), that from time to time desecrate our sanctuaries.

WREATHS, FLORAL DEVICES, ETC.

Cedar, laurel, holly, palm, ground-pine, and box are all used in making wreaths. Where it can be obtained, cedar is certainly the best for the purpose, retaining its color and freshness longer than almost any other greenery, and being more easily worked into shape. Ground-pine comes next in excellence, making a very graceful and airy garland.

The usual method of forming wreaths is to tie sprigs of evergreen on rope, selecting those of uniform size and thickness, and with stems long enough to admit of being securely fastened on, otherwise they will be liable to fall apart when the wreaths are hung in place. Some prefer wire (such as florists use) for fastening the greens on the rope, but twine* is much better, especially if drawn tightly to prevent slipping. Where bunches of holly or other berries are added to the wreaths, when finished wire will then be found useful in holding them in place. It is important that the wreaths be tied as nearly alike as possible, at least such of

---

* Unglazed twine is the best, but if the glazed be used it might be first dipped into water.

them as will be hung together in the decorations, as any perceptible unevenness will mar the
general effect.

For this reason each person might tie enough
for a certain place, using a whole piece of rope,
if necessary, instead of cutting it in shorter
lengths, as many find it convenient to do.

The rope on which these wreaths are made
can be stretched across the room and fastened
each side by means of hooks attached to the
wall (or, if preferred, one end *only* of the rope
may be secured). This holds it firm for the
worker; but most people adhere to the old way
of resting it on their knees as they tie, letting
the ends hang down each side, thus enabling
them to sit in one place,* instead of moving
constantly along, as the former method obliges
them to do.

Each worker could keep a small boy or girl
employed in supplying her with sprays of the
evergreen † ready for putting on. This greatly
facilitates the work. Each person should also
be provided with scissors hanging from her
belt, and gloves might be worn to protect the
hands from contact with the twine and rough
boughs.

---

* A low seat is recommended.

† Bare branches or those which are discolored should not
be used in making wreaths or in any of the decorations.

Wreaths to be used on the altar snould be made, on twine, of delicate sprays of green, so as to resemble foliage. The wreaths as they are finished should be put in a cool place until wanted, as they will wither if left in a warm room.

FLORAL DEVICES

can now be obtained at the florists' at quite moderate prices, though they are not at all difficult to make if one has wire forms on which to construct them. These forms must be filled with wet moss (such as is found in profusion at the roots of maple-trees) held in place with cord crossed over it; and the flowers, after being wired on splints of wood * to lengthen and support the stems, are stuck into the moss according to any arrangement desired.

Baskets and pyramids of flowers can be done in the same manner, and a monogram or motto added, leaving a stripe of plain color through the centre as a ground for it, the letters being put in with small flowers (such as carnations) —white on a scarlet ground, or red on one of lavender. For fine lettering, purple, white, or yellow immortelles are generally used.

Window-slopes can be decorated by having

---

* These can be found at the florists', where wire forms may also be procured.

light wooden or wire frames made to fit them. These are to be filled also with moss, on which a background of flowers of neutral tint may be filled in, and an appropriate motto in large richly colored letters worked into it. A ground of fine green is likewise effective in bringing such mottoes into bold relief, and still another method is to put a layer of black earth or sand into the frames, scattering over it grains of wheat. If placed in the cellar or some other dark place the wheat will come up beautifully in two or three weeks and serve to decorate any part of the church as well as the windows.

It is particularly appropriate for the repository on Holy Thursday, or to adorn the altar on Easter.

In Italy the wheat when grown is put on little ornamental plates or saucers, and a broad ribbon tied around the roots to hold them together. It might, however, be put in small baskets, and the edges trimmed with smilax, or it could be grown in ornamental jars that would do to set on the altar. If exposed to the light a day or two before using it changes from white to a lovely green.

The tin-foil in which floral forms are encased will generally prevent the moisture from damp moss injuring anything with which it may come in contact; but for precaution it is well to have pads of blotting-paper* to use if necessary, or water-proof mats of various sizes might be made by putting thin sheet-rubber between either white or tinted paper.

Baptismal fonts may be beautifully trimmed with ferns, smilax, and flowers. Nothing, however, should be put inside of the font, as it would be a violation of the spirit of the rubric to use it as a flower-vase.†

Wooden crosses four or five feet high, covered with evergreens interspersed with flowers, make a fine decoration for a side wall or niche. A wreath of flowers (made on a barrel-hoop) hung over the top or arm of such a cross is a great addition. Smaller crosses made entirely of ferns fill certain spaces very acceptably. In fact, ferns are used in every manner of decoration nowadays. Boughs and branches of pine can also be used to good advantage, especially in trimming large edifices, where a good display of greens is required. They may be crossed and nailed over doors, on pillars and columns; and in festooning wreaths in any part of the church a cluster of these tasselly branches at each place where the garlands are looped up gives an exceedingly graceful finish.

---

* The layers of thick soft paper that come in boxes of candles are excellent for this purpose.

† It is contrary to the artistic law, as well, to put decorations where they do not properly belong.

Where flowers are scarce, bunches of wheat and scarlet berries are a very good substitute, worked in among the greens. If the berries are difficult to obtain, artificial ones can be made in this way: Take three parts common resin and one part yellow beeswax ;* melt to- gether in a tin or earthen cup, putting in a little powdered vermilion or carmine to color it. Have ready pieces of green-wound wire, five or six inches long, on one end of which a small wad of cotton has been twisted ; dip these into the hot mixture, holding each one a mo- ment after taking out until cool enough to lay down, or else stick them, point downward, into a dish of sand to cool. These berries, placed at intervals among the evergreens, look really better than the natural ones.

An arch covered with evergreens and sur- mounted with a cross might be placed over the chancel gates on high festivals. The cross could be of flowers or gas-jets,† and the arch should bear an appropriate inscription. If sprays of myrtle or smilax ‡ be allowed to de- pend here and there from the arch. it will be the more graceful.

---

* Resin will answer very well without the beeswax.

† Tin sockets for candles can be placed at even distances apart on the top of the arch, where more convenient than gas-jets.

‡ Artificial smilax can be bought by the yard.

Mottoes formed of gas-jets are often seen in Christmas decorations, as is also the star of Bethlehem, which is too familiar a feature to require mention. They should not, however, come in contact with the trimmings, lest the latter might wither or take fire.

TEXTS.

A prominent feature in the decoration of churches is texts or mottoes placed under windows, over doors and arches, and around the gallery. There are, of course, many different kinds of texts, any of which is easily made, however.

One of these consists of illuminated letters on white cloth or paper with a border of evergreens round it, the letters being done in oil or water-colors (having been first drawn with a pencil), care being taken to shade them properly, so they will stand out well. It is a good idea to have an alphabet of large plain letters cut out of cardboard to use as patterns, which if colored after different styles of illumination will serve still better.

Another way is to have a foundation of heavy unbleached cotton cloth on which letters formed of sprigs of evergreen may be sewed. This, if bordered with green, is very effective, the soft tinted ground bringing out the text in fine relief.

It is well to have initial letters of a different color from the others in the texts, as well as a little larger and more ornamental.*

Where a dark ground is desired a piece of boarding of suitable size may be prepared with strips of tape (or cloth) running slanting-wise across it about three inches apart. Under these tapes place the stems of sprigs of green of uniform size, tacking each one down, row after row, until the whole of the board is cov-ered. Illuminated letters can then be fastened on with pins. A rich style of lettering for such a ground can be made by sewing straw of the kind of which hats are made on letters of paste-board, beginning at the outer edge and work-ing toward the centre, thus securing the raised appearance desirable. If properly done they will look equal to gold embroidery. The straw can be procured by the yard at the milliner's.

Gold paper † may be used in covering let-ters, but should be shaded with red or some other color harmonizing with the ground on which they are to be placed.‡ As a variety,

---

* Ferns make a beautiful border for such texts.

† Embossed, not plain, paper should be used.

‡ Harmony should always be considered in the arrange-ment of color.

letters cut from sheet cork may be mentioned. They show to good advantage on a red or blue ground, resembling wood carving. Gold and silver artificial leaves also make beautiful letters for texts or banners.

White letters—showing plainly at a distance —are made by spreading a layer of thick warm paste over a pasteboard foundation and sprinkling it plentifully with rice, letting the grains fall as closely together as possible, although the rougher the surface the better, the intention being to represent carved ivory.

Backgrounds for texts are often made by putting a thin sizing of paste or gum-arabic on heavy white paper, and while wet dusting ground isinglass over it. This, with richly illuminated letters, is very effective in some places.

There are many other fanciful methods of making texts, but they involve a much greater amount of labor than the result compensates for.

Texts suitable for different festivals are too well known to require specifying, but a few are subjoined as suggestions :

Christmas.—" Et Verbum caro factum est." " This day is born a Saviour, who is Christ the Lord." "Gloria in Excelsis Deo." "Behold, I bring you glad tidings of great joy." "And they found Him in a manger." "Lo, the Son of God has come."

Palm Sunday.—"Hosanna to the Son of David." "Blessed is He that cometh," etc.

Easter.—"Ecce Agnus Dei." "I am the Resurrection and the Life." "Christ is risen from the dead." "Alleluia." "He is risen. He is not here."

Whitsunday.—"See the Paraclete descending." "But the Paraclete, the Holy Ghost, whom the Father will send in My name—He will teach you all things."

Corpus Christi.—"Ecce Panis Angelorum." "This is the Bread that came down from heaven." "He that eateth this Bread shall live forever."

Annunciation.—"The angel of the Lord declared unto Mary." "Behold the handmaid of the Lord." "Hail full of grace, the Lord is with thee."

Immaculate Conception.—"Regina sine labe concepta."

Feast of Dedication.—"This is the House which the Lord hath made."

First Communion. — "Feed my Lambs." "Suffer little children to come unto Me."

Confirmation.—"Confirm, O Lord, what Thou hast wrought." "Come, Holy Spirit, Heavenly Dove."

SHIELDS AND BANNERETS

are much used in church decorations, the latter being hung on the walls and pillars, while the former are employed with good effect in festooning greenery. By placing a shield where the wreathing is looped up, it helps to hold it secure, besides serving as an ornament.

These shields may be of thin board or of heavy pasteboard, covered with either gold or colored paper (or with both) put smoothly on. This makes a good ground on which to display floral designs, which can be fastened to the shield with fine wire passed through holes* made for the purpose, and secured on the back.

Where something richer is desired the shield may be covered with velvet, plush, satin, or even cotton-flannel, of colors in strong contrast to the devices which they are intended to display.

For a variety, bouquets of flowers or clusters of callas can be put on some of the shields, instead of having set designs, such as stars, crosses, etc., on them all.

Bannerets can be made of silk, satin, plush, gold cloth, or felt, of different colors, and bordered with gold galloon or with evergreens,

---

* Holes can be made in the shields after they are covered.

according to taste ; a border of ferns or other greens doing very well on felt cloth or cotton-flannel, but scarcely suitable for silk or satin.

They should be about twenty-four inches long and sixteen wide, having inscribed on one side (only) a motto or monogram appropriate to the festival for which they are intended, together with an emblem or picture.*

Bannerets may be lined with cambric and tacked on a pole or curtain-stick, and hung in place with wire. No matter how simple their construction, if in good taste, these bannerets add greatly to the beauty of the decorations, while if more handsomely made with gold trimming, cords, tassels, etc., the effect is increased. A few emblems that would serve for bannerets and shields are here given, together with the corresponding flowers:

Christmas.—Emblem, five-pointed star, called the star of Bethlehem ; flower, holly.

Circumcision of our Lord.—Flower, laurestinus.

---

* Colored lithographs, suitable for different occasions, can be found ready for putting on bannerets. It would be proper to have the episcopal arms of the diocese emblazoned on one banner, the Papal arms on another, while a third one might be decorated with the picture or emblem of the patron saint of the church. These bannerets, however, should be more richly made, to distinguish them from the others.

Epiphany.—Flower, Star of Bethlehem.

Easter.—Emblem, Latin cross; flower, white lily (calla lily). These flowers, if arranged in the form of a cross and used in decorations, have a double signification.

Ascension-day.—Emblem, Latin cross; flower, lily of the valley.

Whitsunday.—Emblem, descending Dove; flower, columbine.

Trinity Sunday.—Emblem, triangle; flowers, Trinity lily (Japanese), herb Trinity, also called pansy; common white trefoil.

Corpus Christi.—Emblem, the pelican; flowers, grapes and wheat.

Holy Cross Day—Emblem, Latin cross; flower, blue passion flower.*

---

* The passion flower is thus described by a Catholic writer : " The leaves represent the spear which pierced our Saviour's side; the tendrils, the cord which bound His hands, or the stripes with which He was scourged: the ten petals. the ten apostles who deserted Him; the pillar in the centre of the flower, the cross; the stamens. the hammers; the styles, the nails; the inner circle about the central pillar, the crown of thorns; the radius round it, the nimbus of glory. The white in the flower is an emblem of purity ; the blue, a type of heaven."

It keeps open three days, and then dies, denoting the death, burial, and resurrection of our Lord.

13

FEASTS OF THE BLESSED VIRGIN

Immaculate Conception—Flower, Arbor vitæ.
Candlemas Day—   "   Snowdrop.
Annunciation (Lady Day)— "   Marigold.
Visitation of the B. V. M.— "   White lily.*
Assumption of the B.V.M.— " Virgin's bower.
Nativity of the B. V. M.— " Bryony, Our
                                  Lady's seal.

FEASTS OF THE SAINTS.

All Saints' Day.—Flowers, sweet bay, dark-red sunflower.

St. Peter.—Emblem, two keys—one of gold, the other of silver—symbolic of the power conferred on him by Christ; flower, yellow cockscomb.

St. Matthew.—Emblem, a book; flower, ciliated passion flower.

St. Mark.—Emblem, a lion; flower, Clarimond tulip.

St. Luke.—Emblem, a calf or young ox; flower, floccose agaric.

---

* The white lily is everywhere recognized as the Blessed Virgin's flower, being typical of her purity, although many other flowers were in ancient times dedicated to her, the marigold especially, which derived its name, so says a writer, "from the fact of its being in bloom on all festivals held in honor of the Blessed Virgin."

CROSSES IN DECORATIONS.

Of the various forms of crosses, those most used in the Church for ornamental purposes are the Latin, Greek, and Maltese, the former being also the episcopal cross, and, as such, worn by a bishop.

Many of the others, however, are appropriate for certain feasts and seasons. For instance, the Tau Cross (also called the Anticipatory Cross) symbolizes the coming of our Saviour, and is used in Advent; while the Greek Cross, as typical of His ministry, may be used in Lent. The Cross of Calvary, which is of the Latin form on an elevation of three steps (representing the three Christian virtues, Faith, Hope, and Charity), is proper for Easter (as well as the plain Latin Cross).

The Triple Cross, having three horizontal bars, is the Pope's cross, and can be used when occasion requires, as also the Cross Patriarchal (having two similar bars), which is the archbishop's cross.

The Cross of Iona, or Celtic Cross,* is appropriate for St. Patrick's Day, as is also the one called St. Patrick's Cross.

---

* A Celtic cross of straw-work on a green shield makes a beautiful decoration for the saint's anniversary.

The Cross of St. George to be used on St. George's Day.

Of all the crosses the Monogram Cross* is the most ornamental.

" It is formed of the two first letters (X and ρ) with which the name of Christ is spelt in Greek. Although called a cross, it partakes more of the character of a monogram. It is sometimes called the Cross of Constantine, because that emperor employed it as a device on his shield and upon his coins. It is found frequently upon the sepulchres in the Catacombs of Rome. It was a symbol much used by the early Christians (this monogram was very often used in writing the name of Christ), and is even found in English documents as late as the year 1493."

This cross is a beautiful device for a banneret or shield.

There are, besides, a great number of other crosses that have no important signification or special appropriateness, save in heraldry, such as the Cross of Jerusalem, St. Anthony's Cross, St. Andrew's Cross, Cross crosslet, Cross *patee*, etc.

---

*Also called the Cross of Constantine.

INDEX.

www.ingramcontent.com/pod-product-compliance
Lightning Source LLC
Chambersburg PA
CBHW030540040726
47497CB00008B/2526